"Durai's clean, news edi
enjoyable to read, and her
done asking hard questions yet.
    —*The Straits Times*

"These ten stories are well-told with sharp, precise prose
and some unexpected ways to look at the role of daily
news in our lives beyond the now-common refrain of
'fake news' and 24/7 clickbait. As a debut collection, it
shows a writer with keen observation and imagination."
    —*Literary Hub*

"Durai unifies this collection around showing us how
newspapers affect characters' lives in different ways.
But journalism itself isn't at the core of these stories;
cultural 'norms' and decorum, defiance, and societal
expectations are."
    —*The Rumpus*

"We read fiction because we enjoy it. Fiction is especially
good for passing time in waiting rooms, on long
commutes, or before falling asleep, and *Regrettable
Things That Happened Yesterday* is adult enough, light
enough, and warm-hearted enough to be excellent for
that purpose."
    —*Singapore Unbound*

"The stories in this gorgeous collection are complex
yet clear, heartbreaking yet hopeful, sharp-witted yet
compassionate. Jennani Durai is an exciting new voice in
literature, a writer to watch!"
    –Tayari Jones, multi-award-winning author of
An American Marriage

"These brisk and clear-eyed stories illuminate both the minor betrayals and the little victories that inevitably define us. Jennani Durai is a disarmingly heartfelt and unpretentious storyteller."

–Cyril Wong, author of *Ten Things My Father Never Taught Me*

"Jennani Durai writes with a confident voice that manages an impressive balance between wry observations and intimacy. Her characters are honestly rendered and they draw the reader into their world with strength and elegance. These stories highlight the pains and triumphs of straddling different cultures."

–Balli Kaur Jaswal, author of *Sugarbread* and *Erotic Stories for Punjabi Widows*

"Jennani Durai's debut collection is a deft work of mixology. These stories are equal part tender stirrings and sharp ripples of humour. She situates in the centre characters who would normally have been peripheral."

–Pooja Nansi, NAC Youth Poet Ambassador and author of *Love is an Empty Barstool*

"*Regrettable Things That Happened Yesterday* presents a series of regrets about being alive and human, before tickling you to death with its sprightly sense of morbid humour. In ten stories centred on the motif of news and reportage, Durai doesn't sugarcoat the everyday tragedies of being a minority in Singapore. Instead she brings you tales of how what is reported is often less than what is said, and far less than what we mean to say–a debut collection of immense skill and wit."

–Ann Ang, author of *Bang My Car*

REGRETTABLE THINGS THAT HAPPENED YESTERDAY

stories

JENNANI DURAI

EPIGRAM BOOKS
SINGAPORE · LONDON

Epigram Books UK
First published by Epigram Books Singapore in 2017
This Edition published in Great Britain in July 2019 by Epigram Books UK

A CIP catalogue record for this book is available from the British Library.

ISBN 978-1-912098-52-1

Printed and bound in Great Britain by Clays Ltd, Elcograf S.p.A.

Epigram Books UK
55 Baker Street
London, W1U 7EU

10 9 8 7 6 5 4 3 2 1

www.epigrambooks.uk

For my husband, my co-conspirator
in making unconventional life plans;
and my mother, who is only slightly
alarmed by them

CONTENTS

INTRODUCTION
BY NG YI-SHENG

I FIRST MET Jennani Durai on Saturday, 23 March 2013, at the launch of *Eastern Heathens* at The Arts House. According to her, our encounter was brief: I went up to her, asked, "Are you Jennani?", thrust a token royalty payment of $20 into her hand, then rushed off elsewhere to worry about logistics.

Despite my ungraciousness, I was actually pretty delighted to make her acquaintance. I'd seen her by-line in *The Straits Times*, and I'd been charmed by the story she'd submitted for the anthology. My co-editor Amanda Lee Koe and I had sent out an open call for short fiction inspired by Asian myths and legends. Most of our submissions were works of fantasy, retelling epic tales of gods and monsters. Jennani's was different: "Tenali Raman Redux" was based on one of the fables of the South Indian jester poet and folk hero Tenali Raman, reimagining him as an incarcerated con-man, still merrily working his plots from behind the walls of Changi Prison.

That story was Jennani's first published work of fiction. Back then, I had no idea that it would lead to a solo collection, the very volume you hold in your hands. What binds this book's stories together is the motif of the newspaper—the eponymous compendium of Regrettable Things That Happened Yesterday—an object that exerts its influence in diverse and subtle ways throughout the book: as the site of horoscopes in "Inexplicably", a story contest in "Yours Truly, Vimala", a job advert in "Revelation to Amala Rose" and movie listings in "PG-13". It even shows how a young woman's pride can end up shredded into kitty litter in "Never Have I Ever".

Yet there's something else that draws these tales together. Perhaps it's because I'm still viewing Jennani's oeuvre through the lens of "Tenali Raman Redux", but I can't help but feel she's a bit of a trickster figure herself, rejoicing in the whimsical absurdities of human experience, cleverly delivering us to unexpected conclusions. Her scenarios are often wonderfully bizarre: in "Funeral Gifts", a dead grandfather is revealed to be a gangster; in "The Employee's Guide to Transporting Customers to Mexico", a restaurant manager pretends that his mixed-race Singaporean waitstaff are Latino. Beneath it all, however, there's an undercurrent of soulfulness: the grief of losing a loved one, the despair of seeing one's dreams come to naught. Tenali Raman may be a master manipulator, but he's still in chains.

Race also plays a part in these stories. These are tales of the South Indian diaspora, principally—though not exclusively—centred on the Singaporean Tamil experience. As ethnic minorities, Jennani's protagonists lead lives informed by tradition and prejudice. Witness how, in "Yours Truly, Vimala", the *Tamil Nesan* valiantly fights to preserve their mother tongue, declaring, "If young people do not start speaking Tamil in social situations, the language will die a painful death with no one left to mourn it." Nevertheless, these characters are not portrayed as victims of their cultural baggage. They have the freedom and agency to befriend and date people of other races. They are intelligent, foolish and flawed. In short, they're human.

Right now, there's a boom taking place in Singaporean short fiction. A new wave of prose writers has hit our shelves: names like Cyril Wong, Alfian Sa'at, O Thiam Chin, Jon Gresham, Victor Fernando R. Ocampo, Amanda Lee Koe and, of course, Jennani herself. They describe our city-state from hitherto unglimpsed perspectives, and our world is far richer as a result. However, this phenomenon would not have been possible without publishers like Epigram Books, who have taken chances on emerging authors, and it could not have thrived without readers like yourself, who are eager to hear these voices.

So thank you for choosing *Regrettable Things That Happened Yesterday*. Jennani's voice is vital, fresh and important. May this be the first of many books to come.

Ng Yi-Sheng
July 2017

FUNERAL GIFTS

IT WAS MY uncle who first made the discovery. As his father's only son, the less-than-pleasant task of ceremonially bathing his corpse had fallen to him. He had wanted to outsource this particular labour of love to the casket company, but my grandmother insisted he do it. When he turned his father over to wash his back, he yelled, dropped my grandfather's lifeless body on the bathroom floor and ran from the room.

I was ordered to retrieve him and so was in a position to confirm it: Thaathaa had a tell-tale tattoo on his left buttock, identifying him as a key leader of a group I had only heard about in whispers at school until now—"BP Pettai", or BPP.

Funnily enough, this was the same group that was said to be behind the parang slashings in Bukit Panjang Park the week before. I mentioned this to my grandmother and received a stinging slap across the face. "Don't be an idiot," she told me. "Only Chinese people have gangs."

She assumed no more would be said on the subject to lend the notion any credence, so when my mother and uncle sat themselves around the table to discuss what, if anything, should be done about this surprising revelation, my grandmother entered a state of denial that would have been acceptable had it not also been belligerent. From her wheelchair, she rapped each of her children across the legs under the table for daring to suggest such an alternate reality, and would have started on me too, if I hadn't cottoned on and addressed her only from afar. My grandmother bellowed that her good husband would be turning over in his grave—had he already been in it—if he could hear what his ungrateful children were now saying about him. Her husband, an honest man who worked hard to provide for their family! She insisted that everyone had misinterpreted what they had seen, that it was not a tattoo but a birthmark, or a liver spot, contoured by the deep wrinkles of nine decades on this earth. What did they know of old age and how a buttock might look after ninety years, she demanded angrily of her children. She asked to be shown the mark, to disprove this theory once and for all, but then started screaming when my uncle approached the corpse to lift his veshti, saying there was no end to the disgrace her evil children would put their dead father through. She might have continued down this path indefinitely for all I know, if the gangsters hadn't started arriving.

The first of them were on our doorstop within the hour. My uncle and I had already sent the casket company workers away, saying that we wanted more time to prepare and dress the body ourselves, and that we would call them closer to the start of the wake. I searched the two young workers' faces for signs that they had spotted the tattoo during the embalming, but they looked nothing but sympathetic. We were all taking turns to shower post corpse contact per my grandmother's instructions when we heard the doorbell. My mother ran to let in the two elderly Indian men, elegantly clad in black Nehru-collared suits with chunky rings on nearly every finger, assuming them to be old friends of her parents. "I'm so sorry, but the wake isn't for another few hours and the casket isn't ready yet," she explained, offering them a seat in our dining room.

"Please don't apologise," one of them said. "We know we are early."

My mother excused herself and left the room to fetch my grandmother, but by the time she had wheeled her in, the guests were gone; the only indication that they had ever been there was a fat envelope of money marked in thick black ink with a symbol we had already seen once that morning, resting on top of the dining room table.

It was not clear which of them started screaming first,

but they both blamed the other for causing my uncle and me to come running. My uncle, who had run out of the shower in a towel with shampoo still in his hair, stared briefly at the envelope before turning to head back to the bathroom, calling over his shoulder to ask his mother if she was convinced yet.

My grandmother, to her credit, managed to calm herself down enough after the initial bout of screaming to wheel herself over to the table—a feat we didn't know she was capable of until now—and reach for the envelope to examine it more closely. "Don't leave fingerprints," said my mother in a screech-whisper, but my grandmother ignored her. She counted all the money, and I waited nearby, hoping she would announce the final tally once she was done, but she slipped the money back into the envelope, and held it in her lap, wordlessly.

She sat in silence until my mother had visibly calmed down too, and then announced that it did not make any sense. "How could I not know," she said, with the intonation of a statement rather than a question, but I guessed that it was a mix of both.

"That Thaathaa was a gangster or that there were gangs at all?" I asked, helpfully trying to clear up the matter, but my mother shut me up with a whack to the side of the head.

"He hid it from us Ma, he hid it from us all," my mother started, but my grandmother interrupted: "He was not that good of a liar. My husband was not like your husband."

"What?" my mother asked faintly, and I was impressed

that even in a moment of betrayal and anguish my grandmother had still found enough malice in her heart to make a jibe about my long-gone father.

My grandmother looked over at me, and then trained her eyes into the distance. "I always knew when he had been with someone else. He would come up with many reasons to explain his lateness, and I would pretend to believe them, but I could always sense a woman's scent on him. I could always tell where he had actually been," she said.

It occurred to both my mother and me that either my grandfather had been the best of liars, inventing one lie to cover another, or that my grandmother had built up an impressive layer of self-delusion. We shared a knowing look but were saved from having to respond by the arrival of more mourners, this time in a group of five or six—youngish men with rat tails and thick gold chains around their necks, who had evidently taken some pains to dress in long-sleeves and button their collars to hide their heavily tattooed bodies. But there was nothing they could have done about the ink on their faces: short, identical lines of dots on their foreheads that even my grandmother could apparently recognise well enough. She sat up straight at the sight of them, and moved as though to get up, before giving up and beginning to cry.

I'd expected her to start yelling again, so the sudden appearance of tears alarmed me. I hurried over and began to wheel her out of the room, making sure to bow my head in an overt gesture of respect to the trained killers who were now traipsing into my family's flat. My mother shot me a look of mixed annoyance and terror at my leaving her alone with them, but she quickly made herself deferential and left also, purportedly to get them cold drinks.

My grandmother was still crying noisily when I wheeled her into her bedroom and shut the door behind us. "It's okay, Paati," I tried, in my best soothing, level voice, even though this was the most exciting thing to ever happen to our family. "You really didn't know. You didn't even know there were Indian gangs in Singapore." I'd thought this would be a comforting thing to say, but as soon as I said it and her head whipped up, I knew I had belittled her further.

She stopped crying momentarily to hiccup a few times in quick succession, evidently the effort of trying to get too much speech out in too short a time. "Now I feel even more stupid," she said, lifting up her shawl to dry her eyes. "All this time I was married to the biggest Indian gangster of them all."

"Well, we don't know that he was the biggest," I said, feeling the situation was getting a little bit away from us, while still enjoying a slight thrill from the thought that I might be the grandson of the feared patriarch of an Indian secret society. Maybe I had even been walking in Bukit Panjang Park one day and some gang members had considered slashing me with a parang, but the older members—those in the know—had restrained them. *That's Ramachandran's grandson*, they might have whispered urgently, *don't even think about touching him.*

I wisely elected not to share this particular fantasy with my grandmother, whose sobs were now fading. She was staring into the distance, her eyes a mixture of despair and resignation. This was the longest conversation I had had with her in as long as I could remember—she spoke only in Tamil, and typically didn't like it when I responded in English, but today she seemed not to mind. I wasn't sure what to do to prolong our conversation, so I suggested going out of the room again, to relieve my mother of the sole responsibility of entertaining our guests.

She looked hesitant. "Did you see the tattoos on their foreheads? I thought only Chinese people had them," she said.

I was already an expert on the subject due to some serious Wikipedia reading this morning, but I was surprised that she knew what the dotted-line tattoos, usually used to mark the fighters, were. "I think they started with Hokkien gangs. They call it *tiam*," I said, but she had already lost interest. "It means they kill people," she intoned. "I won't go out."

I debated bringing up our protected status as the relatives of an influential member of this gang, and the fact that the men in our living room were likely to be front line minions while my grandfather had probably been a behind-the-scenes head-honcho-type. I wasn't sure if she would appreciate this reassurance, so I settled for patting her hand in a comforting manner, and told her I would go check on how my mother was doing.

I'd taken three steps towards the dining room when I

heard my mother usher the last of them out in the fakest cheery voice I'd ever heard. She shut and double-bolted the door, even though we hardly ever had it locked. She saw me and motioned to the table, upon which there was now a new thick envelope, again with the same marking. "Wow," I said, for lack of anything better, and she shuddered and grabbed some tissue, which she used to wrap the envelope before gingerly carrying it to my grandmother. "Fingerprints," she said by way of explanation, and I nodded.

*

By the time the casket company arrived again to set the coffin up for the wake, two more groups of men bearing similar envelopes had come and gone, and my grandmother had thumbed through all of the money, despite my mother's faint protests. She sorted through the money on her bed, facing the wall with her back to us, so I had no chance of spotting the denominations of the bills or guessing at the total tally. My curiosity eventually won out over the deeply ingrained sense that talking about money was vulgar, and I asked.

She shrugged without even glancing at me. "I didn't count. I was just looking at the money to make sure there were no markings on any of the bills."

My uncle heard this as he was walking past and made an exasperated noise in his throat. "Count the money, Dev," he growled at me, and I groaned and dragged my feet as though it wasn't the best order I'd ever received.

My grandmother was surprisingly willing to part with the money, and just stared at me as I moved the wads of cash out of her reach so I could count it.

My first shock was seeing that a $1,000 note of Singapore currency existed, and my second was seeing a $10,000 one. I was now primed for a $100,000 bill and was looking impatiently for one, so the third shock seemed comparatively tame: our total takings so far at Thaathaa's wake were $42,004, and the wake hadn't even actually started.

My grandmother barely batted an eyelid when I informed her of this, so I sought the reaction I desired from my mother, and got it. She shrieked and seemed to be deciding whether the moment called for tears or not, before my uncle said sharply that nothing could be done about it at the moment, and that we should all focus on receiving visitors at the wake, and reconvene to discuss the situation later.

It was clear the casket company workers were not thrilled at the job my uncle had done of dressing my grandfather, and spent a good half-hour silently re-ironing his shirt, arranging his hair and powdering his face. They'd done most of the work in the morning, and the night before— moving all the furniture into one room, draping dark sheets over all reflective surfaces so my grandfather's ghost wouldn't get confused, and setting up an elaborate coffin gilded in gold and precious stones. I thought that was an enormous waste until my mother told me it wasn't the actual box he'd be cremated in. Now they placed his body gently in the casket, and set up a small stand with a picture of him, tea lights and coconuts at his head, and a silver basin full of flower petals at his feet.

The wake itself was fairly uneventful. My mother and grandmother put on old, faded saris so they would look sufficiently bereaved. Apparently only the women needed to dress the part, because my uncle wore a regular office shirt, now stained with nervous sweat. My clothing choice of a STAY HUNGRY STAY FOOLISH: R.I.P. STEVE JOBS T-shirt went entirely unremarked upon.

Far fewer people turned up at the wake than I had expected, although I couldn't quite name specific people who I felt should have cared enough to come. A few relatives were there, scattered among the many Chinese neighbours we barely knew, as well as colleagues of my mother and uncle who were putting in their polite 15 minutes. Some others called to say they would be at the funeral tomorrow. We didn't have all that many relatives in Singapore, as many of my grandparents' siblings had died and their children were mainly in Malaysia. Of those who lived here, many were barely mobile. Still, I would have thought that a death in the family would have made people overcome limitations of mobility or distance and come to comfort my grandmother and her children. I said as much to my uncle, whom I had sort of allied myself with for this occasion—what with our shared history of washing my naked grandfather and all—but he pressed his lips together and said nothing.

When the last visitor left, my grandmother announced

that we all had to shower.

"We are all dirty," she intoned. "From keeping this money the whole day."

My mother sighed and rubbed her temples, as though she had been hoping for a slight break between the wake and the blood money discussion, and my uncle said nothing. I would have liked to take my grandmother up on her suggestion, having shaken hands with and been hugged by far too many people with questionable personal hygiene throughout the day, but the three of them were now circling each other in the living room, as though sizing one another up before making their decision.

My mother and uncle took their seats, and my grandmother wheeled her chair around to face them. "We will call the police," she said simply, the matter decided.

"No," shot back both siblings. They started talking at once, and for some reason the conversation shifted entirely into Tamil.

"This money was a gift to us."

"We can't tell the police about who Appa was."

"We're not even sure what we think we know is definitely true."

"We may get implicated in all this."

"People give us gifts and we get them in trouble?"

"It will tarnish his reputation forever; what will all your friends and relatives say?"

In addition to not being able to tell who was saying what, I also was not entirely sure what was being said and was straining to catch every word. My grandmother put an end to it by brandishing her stick and bellowing over them: "Just think about how the money was made, it was bought with the lives of people!"

My uncle winced and motioned for her to lower her voice. My mother remained undeterred. "We don't know how that money was made," she said. "We don't know what they do."

I wasn't sure if she was supporting her brother or her mother, but this was one question I did have the answer to. I started reciting the litany of BPP's activities I had found on its Wikipedia page: "Loan shark running, drug running, territory-marking activities, intimidation activities and occasional weapon-assisted violence," I said, proud of myself for being able to contribute, before the startled look in my mother's eyes told me that they had all forgotten I was there.

"Even the boy knows," screeched my grandmother. "Is this the kind of example you want to set for your son?"

"Oh, I don't mind," I started saying, but then decided I should just back out of it.

My uncle took control. "Okay, sure, let's give back all the money to the police," he said. "A funeral is a lot of money, but usually a family has some help to pay for a funeral, some monetary gifts their friends and family are thoughtful enough to give. Did many of your relatives come today, Ma? To show their support? To offer their help?"

I hadn't been sure whether only I had noticed, but the way the room fell silent proved otherwise. To my surprise, this stopped my grandmother's rampage in its tracks, and she now bit her lip as tears filled her eyes.

"Oh Ma, I'm sorry," my uncle started and moved as though to comfort her, but she waved him away.

Everyone waited for her to dry her eyes and speak again, and in the interim I may have fallen asleep. I woke when my grandmother uttered the only curse word in Tamil I knew, which never in my life had I heard pass her lips. We sat straight up in the newly charged silence in the room as my uncle and mother exchanged looks to decide who would speak next. If my grandmother was embarrassed by her sudden loss of verbal control, she didn't show it, sitting back in her chair and crossing her arms as if daring someone to speak, to refute the sentiment that she had just expressed about their family.

My mother unfortunately took the bait. "They might have been busy," she said, and her droopy eyelids indicated she didn't completely realise what she was saying, but that didn't stop my grandmother from starting her second outburst in less than five minutes.

"Busy?" she yelled. "Busy with what, sitting on their butts the whole day because they are too fat to stand up? Those dogs, those pieces of shit couldn't come for my husband's wake? Their own relative—when I die are they going to do this too? Make a phone call and pretend to say nice things while being too *busy* to leave their stupid house to come for a wake? I hope one of them dies next, I hope they all die one after another very quickly so I can sit here and watch and not go to a single one of their wakes—"

"Okay Ma, I was just trying to give them the benefit of the doubt," my mother started, trying to talk over my grandmother, but then just giving up. She stood up and looked around at all of us. "I'm going to bed," she said. "You all do what you want with the money."

"I think we all need to go to bed," said my uncle as my mother left the room. "We're all tired, we're still upset about Pa, and we're disappointed in our family. This isn't the time to decide about the money."

I agreed, although it felt like a cop-out. I expected my grandmother to break into another outburst, but she just sat there and said nothing.

As I turned off the lights in the living room and started wheeling her out, she suddenly said: "I wonder why they— those gangsters—came before the wake started. We put the time in the notice, you know."

I'd thought this was obvious. "I mean, they're gangsters, right? Someone might have called the police," I said. I didn't add: *You* might have called the police.

I helped her wash her face and get ready for bed, a task my mother normally did but seemed to have abandoned for tonight. "That's a pity," she said quietly as I helped her into bed, and I wasn't sure I'd heard her right, but was too tired to inquire further.

*

The next morning, I woke up to the sound of my mother screaming. By the time I had stumbled into the dining room, my uncle—who had spent the night on our couch—was standing over the open *Tamil Murasu* that was the source of my mother's consternation.

The newspaper was open to the Obituaries section. Just the day before, we had placed a small 6cm-by-8cm black-and-white notice about my grandfather's wake and funeral. Today, however, his larger-than-life countenance stared back at us from a full-page coloured obit.

The picture used was one we had never seen before: in it, my grandfather is not smiling as I always remembered him, but his mouth is set in a straight line and hidden beneath his thick moustache. His eyes are piercing, his hair neatly combed back, and a thick gold chain peeks out from beneath the stiff shirt collar of his sombre black suit, as if donned to mourn himself.

The words were simple: "Always in our hearts. We continue what he started."

I looked nervously at my mother, who had moved from shock to an almost-wry disbelief. "And if that were not enough to tell the whole world exactly who he was," she said, and flipped the page. "This should remove any lingering doubt."

On the next two pages were six more iterations of the same image of my grandfather, in varying sizes, some in colour and some black and white, each with its own inscription. The inscriptions themselves were tame—most were variations of "RIP" or "Always in our hearts", again— but they were followed by different strings of initials, and then: BPP.

"Ah," said my uncle, and that was really all that could

be said.

My grandmother was wheeling herself slowly into the living room, and my uncle tried to block the newspaper from her view, but my mother just grabbed the newspaper and handed it to my grandmother. "What's the point in hiding it?" she asked her brother. "Like I said, the whole world knows."

My grandmother stared at the full-page picture of her late husband with her lips parted, as though she could not quite recognise his face when blown up to such proportions. She flipped between that and the pages with the smaller pictures slowly, repeatedly.

In the silence, my uncle said: "I can't believe the *Tamil Murasu* let them just take out obituaries. Isn't it against the law?"

I asked hopefully: "Maybe this means that BPP isn't a universally recognised acronym?"

My mother shut us up: "You think that stupid newspaper is going to turn away anyone's money?"

I kept my eyes on my grandmother, who still hadn't spoken yet that morning after her loquacity the night before, and soon we all were staring at her in silence, the only sound in the room the slow flipping of newspaper.

Finally she looked up and I swear she had tears in her eyes. "They really loved him," she said.

*

The funeral was at Mandai Crematorium and a priest—part of the package we had paid for at the casket company—

showed up at our flat at 9am sharp to chant some mantras and then accompany us there. The whole thing could have been done in our flat, but my grandmother had somehow convinced my uncle to spring for the Platinum package with the casket people, which came with a hall at Mandai in addition to some extra priest time and the ruby-encrusted coffin. My uncle had asked to do the funeral the day before, right after the wake, but the priest had refused, saying he would not conduct a funeral on a Saturday. My mother and uncle were not in a position to object, being completely unversed in the best practices for sending a loved one to the afterlife, and we spent one last night in our flat with my grandfather.

The priest, a skinny prune of a man, arrived dressed to impress: a traditional veshti around his waist, a string taut and diagonal across his bare chest, and every manner of ash and pigment smeared across his forehead. My grandmother seemed mollified by how very holy he appeared, and squeezed his hand and beamed up at him when he approached to give her his condolences.

The funeral itself was short: sandalwood paste applied to our foreheads, prayers sung by the priest, last rites that my uncle had to carry out that he didn't know about, and an uncomfortably empty hall.

During the car ride to the crematorium, my grandmother had stressed to me how important it was in Hindu funerals for the family not to be seen welcoming the other mourners but to instead be lost in their own grief. But she turned around in her seat every thirty seconds during the funeral to see if anyone had arrived to pay their final respects. When it became clear that the priest had finished and was eyeing us for clues as to what to do next, my grandmother closed her eyes and let out a long, sad sigh.

"I'm so sorry, Ma," said my uncle, putting an arm around her.

"It might have been the *Tamil Murasu*," mused my mother. "They must have seen the obituaries and decided to stay away."

"It wasn't the obituaries," said my grandmother. "Please, let's finish so I can go home."

My mother and uncle walked on ahead with the priest as workers from the crematorium came in to take the coffin on its final journey. I wheeled my grandmother to the casket so she could say her final goodbye to her husband. She put her fingers against the glass covering his face. "I'm sorry," she said softly. And then, to me: "Let's go."

I pushed her wheelchair into the connecting room, following the clearly demarcated route to the viewing chamber. I already had a queasy feeling in my stomach. It was my first time at Mandai and this final part, where the family is expected to watch as their loved one's coffin goes through the flames, struck me as the most perverse of all. I deliberated wheeling my grandmother into the chamber and then excusing myself, but I stopped short when I got to the small, dark room and found it full.

My mother and uncle were standing in the middle of the chamber, looking simultaneously bewildered and terrified, while at least thirty members of BPP, dressed in almost identical black shirts and white veshtis, milled around them. Some were in wheelchairs and some had the dotted forehead tattoos that had so frightened my grandmother at first, but they all turned reverentially towards her now as we entered the room. All at once, they raised their hands, palms pressed together at their chests as if to say *vanakkam*. I spotted two familiar, impassive faces: the casket company workers. I felt a sudden rush of gratitude.

I pushed my grandmother's wheelchair into the centre of the room, and she motioned to me that she would like to stand. I helped her up, grabbing one of her arms while my uncle quickly grabbed the other. She walked slowly towards the black-clad man closest to her, one of the younger ones with forehead ink, clasped his hand and shook it. She turned slowly and did the same with the man next to him.

The BPP members slowly formed a semicircle around us as they realised what was happening. It took almost twenty minutes but my grandmother managed to shake hands with them all.

The crematorium attendant had been watching respectfully, and as she shook hands with the last of the members who had come, my grandmother nodded towards him that she was ready.

She shuffled back into the centre of the circle and let go of my hand and my uncle's, taking hold of the hands of two BPP members instead. I followed her lead and so did the rest of my family, and then we all stood hand in hand, shoulder to shoulder, the people who knew my grandfather best in this world, as we watched his body burn.

INEXPLICABLY

INEXPLICABLY, THE FIRST thing she thought of was her mother's advice never to turn down a gift.

She felt that now was not the right time to remember this, a hastily issued rejoinder from when she was nine and upset that she had received Mumbai Barbie instead of Malibu Barbie at a Christmas party. She also felt a little let down by the universe and any deities that might govern it, that this should be what entered her mind when she had just been proposed to.

Her second thought was that the little box between Arun's thumb and forefinger was too blue—not Tiffany

& Co blue, but blue in a way that suggested the makers hoped you might mistake it for Tiffany. Maya made no such mistake, but despaired again that her thoughts seemed insistent on not focusing on the one issue that really needed her attention.

They had been walking down State Street and she had stopped at a hippie store to buy a "Green for Life" bumper sticker on a whim. She had been meticulously sticking it onto the back window of Arun's Ford Escape, being careful not to trap any air bubbles under it while wondering briefly if it was hypocritical to be affixing that sentiment to such a gas guzzler, when she noticed out of the corner of her eye that Arun was kneeling on the ground.

She swivelled and tried to keep her obvious alarm out of her face as he asked her in his quiet, steady voice to marry him. He didn't add anything else—none of that "I know this is really sudden", or "You would make me the happiest man in the world". His request was plain, direct and exactly what she would have expected of him, had she expected him to propose.

They had met only four months ago, at a meeting of Singaporean students at the University of Wisconsin–Madison. She was a junior studying journalism and attending only her second-ever Singapore Society meeting, having deftly avoided them until she was cornered on the way to Econ 201 by the society president and made to promise she would attend the Chinese New Year get-together. Arun was a first-year graduate student, studying mathematics. Typical, she had thought when he'd introduced himself to the group, but he was strangely magnetic. He could be surprising, she thought, just as he flashed her a shy smile. They were the only two ethnically Indian students there, and as much as she was desperate to avoid stereotypes, desperate to date outside her race, she felt some sort of attraction to him.

She hadn't wanted to date an Indian; she never had in Singapore and hadn't planned to upon coming to the States. And a Singaporean Indian, of all people—she might as well have let her mother set her up.

He had asked her later that night if she would like to meet for coffee and she found herself agreeing. That coffee date turned into him bringing her Starbucks when she was up late studying, which soon turned into them making meals together on weekends, which soon turned into them waving tentatively at each other's parents on Skype video chats, which soon turned into Maya's star sign being included in the Tamil newspaper horoscope clippings Arun's mother sent him by mail every month. And now it had turned into a full-fledged proposal on a busy corner of State Street, where passers-by had stopped to watch, forming a huddle of around fifteen people who were alternately exclaiming and sighing. To Maya, it seemed like the street itself had paused and inhaled, and was looking to her now for the cue to breathe again.

She looked down at Arun, who appeared to be his normal self—stoic, impassive, logical—and knew that he was quite serious. He was always serious, a trait of his she had thought would be a deal-breaker at first, a hindrance to her free spirit, but it was one she had slowly grown to accept and even respect. He was so serious that she wondered why he had even attempted this public proposal, when he must know that the possibility of her saying no was very real. They had only been dating for four months, after all. She wondered if he was under some kind of pressure from his family that he had kept from her, or if the latest horoscope clipping had suggested that prolonged singleness might be injurious to his health. Her mind was drifting back to her mother's words, when Arun began to speak again.

"There are a lot of people watching," he said, surprising Maya by speaking in Tamil. They had only ever spoken in English these past few months, as if by an unspoken pact. She had always appreciated it, as if they were saying to each other, *Hey, we're dating because we're people who like each other, regardless of being of the same ethnic and language group.* He continued: "If you're going to say something other than yes, could you please say it in Tamil?"

Relief bloomed slowly in the pit of her stomach as his words registered, and she wondered if he had just thought of this, or if this was part of the plan from the beginning. Knowing him, he had calculated his actions and words precisely, down to a science, and this was his Plan B should she hesitate for more than x number of seconds.

She wondered how long she had been standing there speechless, and quickly rehearsed her answer in her mind—her Tamil was rusty, and she didn't want to make any mistakes. She would ask her mother later if this instance might be an exception to the cardinal rule, but now she bent down a little and took his familiar face in her hands. She looked deep into the eyes she both knew so well and didn't know at all. She drew the corners of her mouth upward, made her eyes twinkle, and responded in Tamil: "I don't know."

She braced herself for the disappointment to seep into his eyes, but Arun seemed prepared for exactly this response, judging from the speed with which a smile spread across his face.

He jumped to his feet, pumped one fist into the air, and they hugged, as applause broke out all around them.

YOURS TRULY, VIMALA

THE CONTEST HAD been going on for as long as Prema could remember. Her father would come home after his morning walk every Sunday with a copy of the *Tamil Nesan* and her sisters would pounce on various sections of it—Indian cinema gossip, fashion, advice, horoscopes. She would join in on this activity only once a month, on the first Sunday, when she would jostle with the rest to get a hold of the paper while it was still crisp, extracting the one page that held any interest for her.

It said the same thing each time: DO YOU LOVE STORIES? DO YOU LOVE THE TAMIL LANGUAGE?

ARE YOU A STUDENT 18 YEARS OR YOUNGER? SHOW US YOUR TALENT BY ENTERING THE TAMIL NESAN YOUNG WRITERS STORY CONTEST TODAY!

And then, in smaller print: UNDER 2,000 WORDS.

It was followed by a prompt for that month's story. Usually a topic sentence—"If young people do not start speaking Tamil in social situations, the language will die a painful death with no one left to mourn it"—or a concept—"sibling rivalry"—or a scene—"A two-storey attap house sits in the middle of an abandoned street. The street lamp in front of it has ceased working for a few years now. All the plants in the garden are dead. Stray dogs roam about the road, but even they do not stop at the house."

Prema tried every month. She had a stack of A4-sized envelopes on her desk, already stamped and addressed to the *Tamil Nesan* head office in Kuala Lumpur, just waiting for a newly-minted story to be slotted into them and mailed off. She had a system. She spent the first week of the month working on the story, the second week reading it over and revising it heavily, the third week making final edits and sending it off. The fourth week of the month was spent reading other short stories to get ideas and be inspired, and pretending not to be awaiting news of successful acceptance and imminent publication.

In that fourth week, she read short stories in any language she could find—English, for the best ideas; Malay, to keep doing well in school while waiting to get her big break; Tamil, to "constantly have the sound of excellent Tamil in her ear" as she wrote her soon-to-be-award-winning entries (she had heard that statement in one of Meena Rajendran's weekly interviews with a published author, "Stories of Success"—Sunday nights at 8pm only on Minnal 96.8FM, Tamil Hits All Day).

The selected winners were published in the paper two months after the prompt was originally announced, and sometimes their stories would even be read out on the radio. She read these winners' stories religiously, often whisking the paper away to her room so she could read slowly, forming her lips into each word as she read, trying to discern some rhythm, some flow, some depth, vocabulary, inventiveness, richness, humour, moral or whimsicality that those stories possessed and hers hadn't.

She made notes. She underlined phrases she liked and would try to use again, she tacked up the most interesting stories on her door, she put the stories she didn't quite like into her bottom drawer so she would not be influenced by them despite their apparent award-winning quality (she wanted to write what she herself would read—another tip from Meena's interviews). She kept a notebook of ideas and phrases and ways to improve, as well as motivational quotes so she would not give up.

Her behaviour worried her mother, tickled her sisters and even garnered mild notice from her father. Any attention was good news: Prema was sixth in a line of seven children, six unsuccessful attempts for a boy before Lucky Number 7 yielded the desired result. As such, all parental attention was currently focused on Mano, the darling baby of the family, the long-awaited heir and hope for the future. He was currently nine and not very friendly, a trait that all the sisters privately blamed their parents for.

With ninety per cent of their parents' attention thus occupied, Prema had to fight for the remaining ten per cent. This was not as hard as it might have seemed from the outset. The two oldest, Kalai and Chithra, were in their thirties, married, and had moved out for a few years now. They both lived in Singapore with their husbands, a fact that their mother deplored and their father was quietly proud of. The two next oldest—Sumathi the docile one, and Malathi, the vain one—had been shipped off to a British-style boarding school just north of KL. Prema saw them even less than she saw her oldest sisters. She felt slightly bad that every time someone asked her what her sisters' names were, she always remembered Malathi and Sumathi last.

That left just Prema, 14 years old and not planning on leaving home any time soon, and Vimala, 18 months older but whom Prema felt liked to act younger whenever she felt Prema was getting too much parental attention.

The fact was, Prema never got too much attention. She believed her mother had been sapped of energy by the time she came along, and left the task of raising her mostly to her two oldest sisters. Her father had probably glanced at her once as a newborn and, upon ascertaining that she really was yet another girl, turned his disappointed gaze away, never to be coaxed back. (This was at least how it played out in her mind; she hoped one day to write a story about it or include it as a dramatic chapter in her heart-breaking memoir of an unloved child who turned into a much beloved author. Proceeds of the autobiography would go to orphans in Southeast Asia: "Those as unloved now as I was then", she would write in the inscription.)

She'd had five years of half-hearted indifference from her parents when Mano came along. Suddenly her mother, recently forty, got a second wind and her father, pushing fifty, became excited about parenthood.

For a while, that energy encompassed Prema, too: Mano's arrival reminded her parents that they'd had another baby not too long ago, and they made an effort. Her mother's labour with Mano had been a hard one, and both mother and son were kept in the hospital for nearly two weeks for observation. When Prema came to visit, her mother would quiz her anxiously: had she eaten? Were her sisters taking care of her? Were they all being nice to each other? Was Kalai taking her to school every day? And Prema would answer them all dutifully, although the answers never differed.

"Where's Prema?" her father would grandly ask whenever they left the house to load into the Morris Minor to go to the hospital. This thrilled her inordinately, and she would push her way to the front of the group of sisters and wave her hand in the air as if to say, *Here I am!* He would smile at her, amused by her excitement, pat her on the head and hold her hand until they got to the car. This was the extent of his concern for her wellbeing, however, because the minute Baby Mano was in sight her father forgot all his previous children and became consumed with his son like a first-time father.

They had not been entirely remiss. It was her father, for instance, who made sure that all his daughters were educated in the three languages—Malay to survive until they could escape Malaysia, English to survive once they were out of Malaysia, and Tamil for their mother, who refused to learn any other language.

It was also her father who had introduced her to the ballpoint pen. To Prema's mind, the ballpoint pen was the pinnacle of human inventiveness. The day her father brought home a Bic from the office for her was a day she'd remember all her life—how she had handled it so carefully, afraid to drop it, and then inevitably dropping it due to her cautiousness. But it had kept on writing, producing ink continuously without needing to be dipped into a pot of Quink, without leaving ink stains on her hands or smudges on her paper. It was a miracle. It would never run out. She would use the same pen forever.

The total tally of stories Prema had submitted to the *Tamil Nesan* contest stood at either 30 or 31—depending on whether you counted one revision she had sent in. At the beginning, they used to send her a letter of acknowledgement that she thought was quite nice. "Dearest Miss Prema Chandran," it would read. "We thank you for your most promising contribution to the *Tamil Nesan* Young Writers Contest. We will review your entry along with all the others, and winners will be announced in a month's time. Thank you for reading *Tamil Nesan*."

But after her fifteenth or sixteenth entry, the letters stopped. This greatly puzzled Prema as she had grown to enjoy these little notes, and as sad as she knew this to be, she was depending on that one word—"promising"—as the only affirmation she was getting for her writing.

She let it slide the first month, but the second month she didn't get a letter, she called the head office in KL, worried that they hadn't received her entry. A clerk answered, sounding unenthusiastic, and put her through to the person in charge of the contest, a Miss V. Rani. (Prema made a mental note to memorise the name and insert it as the name of a beautiful young protagonist in her next story.)

Miss V. Rani answered politely and apologised for the missing letter, explaining that there had been a paper shortage in the office that month, but that yes, she had in fact received an entry from one Prema Chandran, 27B Jalan Kembagan, Klang, and one the month before. She thanked Prema for her "top-class monthly contributions", and told her that the office might be tight on paper for the rest of the year, so would it be okay if they stopped sending her acknowledgements?

Highly gratified that the *Tamil Nesan* head office knew her name and the frequency of her contributions to the contest, Prema had accepted the explanation. "Let the newer writers get the letters, that is fine. You don't have to send me more," she said grandly, and hung up after thanking V. Rani profusely. She took out her notebook and wrote "Top-class contributions—Miss V. Rani of

Tamil Nesan", and tore out the page to fold into a little square to keep in her wallet. That way she could take it out once a month to read with pride in lieu of the acknowledgement letter.

Affirmation of any kind was rare in their household, and Prema doubted any of her family even knew what it was. What she couldn't figure out was why none of them seemed to need it as much as she did. Her parents seemed to be independent operators, self-sufficient and requiring nothing from each other or their children. The last compliment she had probably heard pass from one to the other was that the lentil curry was tastier than usual today.

Of her siblings, she suspected that the one who felt the closest to the way she did was Vimala, with her occasional pretences of being younger than she really was. The cutesy act grated on Prema's nerves, but at least was evidence that she was not alone in craving more attention. She tried to bring up this similarity to Vimala a few times, to suggest that perhaps they could confide in each other, encourage each other and be the closest of the sisters. But Vimala had a confusing quality that Prema could not figure out. She felt sometimes that Vimala was her favourite sister because of how effortlessly they got along when they were alone, but she would change completely and become someone else's best friend when there was any other person in the room. She was a chameleon, and Prema did not know what to make of that.

The lack of positive reinforcement in her household would normally have just been something to sigh briefly over every once in a while, were it not for her current situation. She needed a reader (said Meena). She needed constructive criticism to improve, yes, but she also needed someone to point out her strengths and remind her every once in a while why she felt a calling to put pen to paper in the first place (quoted almost verbatim from one of Meena's interviews and copied carefully into her notebook). Vimala would have been the obvious choice, but her changing moods and personalities made for an inconsistent reader, and she'd likely give mixed, confusing feedback.

Sometimes she would try to bring up the topic of her stories around the dinner table, drawing a similarity between one of her sisters and a character in her story, or remarking that a piece of dialogue was so funny, she would have to use it in one of her stories. But hardly anyone picked up on what she considered to be blatant offers to let someone read her work. Mano had expressed some interest once, and in her desperation she let a nine-year-old read one of her stories, a mistake she vowed never to repeat again. He took a red pen to it and wrote comments like *"I don't get it. Was this supposed to be funny?"*, *"Why is this character so irritating?"* and *"Sounds like Enid Blyton, you copycat."*

The story that Mano had read had been Prema's 28th contribution to the *Tamil Nesan*. She felt that her time was soon coming. Her characters were more developed, her vocabulary better and her themes more varied—she had even included some romance in her last two stories, something she had never before attempted. She had thought that she would describe a romantic relationship too unconvincingly, given that she had never been in one before, but she decided that she would attempt it after the winning entries for the past couple of months had revolved around themes of love. If the contest judges were on a romance kick, she didn't want to ignore it and give them the idea that she did not closely benchmark her writing to the previously published pieces.

So she tried her hand at love stories. Nothing too risqué, lest Miss V. Rani and her ilk at the *Tamil Nesan* have their sensibilities offended—just some hand-holding, some pronouncements of love, and one extended scene in which the protagonists stare so long into each others' eyes that they see the other's soul.

The love stories suffered the same fate as their predecessors, that is, they were not published, but Prema remained convinced of their inherent value, and felt it made her future testimony all the more impressive. "I tried 28 times before I was finally published," she would say to Meena when she herself was finally interviewed at that sacred 8 o'clock hour on Sunday nights. Her rehearsed speech altered slightly every month with each new non-publication, making the "interview" all the more heart-wrenching and dramatic, she thought.

Her 31st story was her magnum opus (thus far: she hoped to have more opuses, or was it opii? She would have to check). It was part-desperation, part-inspiration. Between Mano's dismissive comments, her own fears of sounding like she was rehashing someone else's original material, and the fact that she had now submitted thirty manuscripts without success, she knew she was on the verge of losing all self-belief and perhaps even giving up altogether. She voiced this fear to Vimala, but unfortunately caught her in one of her less pleasant moods, because Vimala agreed with her, and said she would have given up a long time ago if she had received rejection upon rejection.

The word "rejection" was what Vimala used—not Prema. She had never thought of her lack of success as "rejection" exactly, and she was startled to hear it now. She had simply thought that one month, she would win. And the months when she hadn't, it was just someone else's time to win. Sure, she had been disappointed—especially after submitting her first few stories, she had been sure they were winners—but she had come to so enjoy the whole process, from anticipating the theme, to waiting for her father to come back with the newspaper, to thinking of a plot, to putting it down on paper, and seeing a whole story formed from nothing more than a prompt of a couple of words and her own imagination. She didn't win, but she had never thought that her work was not good, or that it had been "rejected".

So Vimala's comment had disturbed her, which accounted for her new desperation to get the *Tamil Nesan* to take notice of her and publish her writing. But she was also more excited and confident of success than usual because she had what she thought was her best story yet. Part-memoir and part-fiction, her newest story, sparked off by the ingeniously vague *Tamil Nesan* prompt "celebrating differences", she would write a story about the most different people she knew—her family.

She took pains to disguise her family members in the story on the chance that she did get published and they recognised themselves portrayed unfavourably. She changed names and appearances, and added two extra siblings. She gave them all English names and situated the story in London, which was believable, because she had an aunt and an uncle there, and they said there were all sorts of Tamil people over there. And she made them Christians. She made the youngest child the narrator, a girl born just after a long-awaited boy child, who stayed largely in the shadows and observed the dynamics of the family, all the while making notes about how she would run her own family one day.

The story took longer than her others had. She was still not done with it by the middle of the second week, which made her worry she wouldn't have time to revise it and send it in before the deadline. But when she finally finished it (six days later than usual), she felt so satisfied that she believed hardly any revisions were going to be necessary. She did edit it for grammar, but left her plot and dialogue largely unchanged, feeling it did justice to the odd balance of comedy, dysfunction and conservativeness of her family—while giving no hint that she was actually talking about them, of course.

The story ended with the precious son dying in a tragic traffic accident and the family, in the midst of their grief and shock, realising they had another child they never paid attention to, who was now, as a result of that deficit, scrawny from being under-fed, but brilliant in all other aspects.

In a tear-jerking conclusion, the negligent parents and the overshadowed daughter embraced, and the father made a half-page monologue vowing to spend the rest of his life making it up to her, while the other siblings looked on in a mixture of envy, awe and camaraderie.

The ending was so good that Prema herself shed a few tears while writing it—not so much for the dead son as for the triumph of the unassuming underdog (also, she was quite taken with the unprecedented poetry of her prose). She had heard that many writers got emotionally involved like this with their characters—she imagined they often penned the last word and collapsed into tears, re-reading the last paragraph several times, as if hoping somehow to extend it and stave off the moment when the story would be over.

It was almost how she felt that Sunday night, when she turned on the radio a few minutes earlier than Meena's usual time slot, and recognised the words being read out as her own. She gasped and turned the volume up so that she could hang on to every word, her moment that had arrived so unceremoniously. Read out over the radio, the story seemed more impressive than ever, and she marvelled once again that she had written it. She felt jolts of impatience when the reader's tone did not rise and fall as she had written it, or when emphases were misplaced, but these flitted in and out of her mind in an instant, in her nervous anticipation for the reader to get to the next word, and the next after that. The voice was high and over-articulate, probably a special voice reserved for reading in public that would sound nothing like the reader's normal speech, but Prema was happy enough that it was clear, and hundreds, maybe thousands of listeners across Malaysia were now hearing the story that Prema had conceived and written, hanging on to every word and eager to hear how it all ended.

So intent was she on not missing a word that she hadn't thought to call any of her family members to come listen, and now as the story reached its climax she was suddenly gripped by the thought that there was no one to witness her glory. Unlike a notice in a newspaper, the words over the radio were slipping away every second.

"Amma!" she called, not wanting to leave the big radio in the living room, but she didn't know if her voice would carry to her mother in the kitchen. "Amma? Appa?" No response, so she tried: "Vimala akka?" And against all reservations, desperate: "Mano?"

As luck would have it, her brother popped his head in immediately, as if waiting for her to say his name. "What?" he said, mildly interested at being addressed after having been ignored by Prema since his blistering critique of Story #28.

"It's my story," she told him excitedly, jabbing towards the radio. "My story is being read out," she said.

He walked over to the radio and sat himself down cross-legged next to it, an intent look on his face, and he glanced over at Prema curiously.

"Just in time," she said. "It's ending."

The teary dialogue at the end was wrapping up, and Prema sat back as the last line was read, satisfied, only to jerk up as she heard the next thing the reader said.

"Thank you for listening to my story titled 'Celebrating Differences'," said the reader in a still clear but now less forced and more familiar-sounding voice. "This is yours truly, Vimala Chandran."

Afterward, she would tell her sisters that the feeling that overcame her was one of an immediate fury that caused a temporary blindness, as if a white-hot skewer had been pressed down into her eyes, causing the world to appear like a bright, hot space that was suffocating her.

But the truth was that she remained sitting still for a long time—back erect, head cocked at an angle, eyes focused straight ahead on the radio, lips parted and brows wrinkled. The current programme had ended and the next was starting—the one she had originally turned on the radio to listen to—but she didn't notice. The parting words of the previous voice on the radio were repeating themselves in her head, and she was trying desperately to understand them. In fact, her first coherent thought was that they must have mispronounced her name, that somehow the reader, intending to say that the story was written by one Prema Chandran, had flubbed, accidentally saying "Vimala" when she meant "Prema". Perhaps the reader had the name "Vimala" on the brain.

It was Mano who reacted first. He jumped up, and in

the quickness of his movement nearly fell over backward. On his face was etched pure indignation, and he stared at Prema furiously, like a soldier looking to his general for the command to fire. As the seconds stretched and Prema still sat there with her unreadable expression, he ran over to her and grabbed her arm, as if trying to jolt her into action.

"Prema akka," he cried, his voice the high-pitched hiss of one who has been personally wronged. "Vimala akka stole your story!"

Mano's proclamation, strong, sure of itself and leaving no room for an alternative explanation, snapped Prema out of her temporary trance.

"What?" she asked, although the real question her brain was struggling to ask was more along the lines of "how?" or really "why?"

Mano put his hands on her shoulders. "Prema akka," he enunciated slowly, looking her dead in the eye as if it might aid her comprehension. "Vimala akka stole your story."

He frowned. "How do you usually submit your stories?" he asked.

Prema was struggling to string a sentence together. "I mail them in," she said. "I put them in an envelope, ask Appa for a stamp, and then the next time we go into town I'll mail it."

"And you always do this yourself?" asked Mano, not convinced.

No, Prema did not always do this herself. She often just

asked whoever was going into town to mail it for her. But this was too hard to articulate at the moment—she could have cried for letting this happen. But how was she to have known?

"Sometimes I ask Appa," she said weakly.

"Sometimes," Mano repeated. "Or you could have asked anyone else who was going into town, am I right?"

For the life of her, Prema could not remember. She could have asked Vimala, yes, but she could have asked any other sister, and with so many of them, who could keep track? Who could remember which sister she asked to mail which story? She stared mutely back at Mano, who was now shaking his head with a look of immense sympathy on his face. He then turned and bolted out of the room.

"Amma!" he screamed. "You need to hear what Vimala akka did, now."

The conversation that ensued did not quite register in Prema's brain. She didn't leave the room, but sat there in the same spot, listening to the unfolding commotion in the kitchen where Mano had accosted their mother. She remembered knowing that all her sisters had gathered around them to listen to what Mano was saying, because of the numerous interjections from different voices. She remembered her mother distractedly repeating, "Oh dear, oh dear", while Sumathi clucked disapprovingly (soft) and Malathi clucked disapprovingly (loud), and Kalai, who had just arrived from Singapore, said, "Oh our poor Prema" twice and "What can that Vimala be thinking?"

three times.

And she remembered Mano, spoilt little brother Mano, who had not known tact or constructive criticism, and whom she had not talked to for three months, but who was now screaming bloody indignant murder at the wrongness of it all.

She felt a vague wave of guilt for killing his character counterpart in the story at the centre of the current upheaval, even in the midst of the hurt, confusion and non-comprehension that had lodged themselves into her brain.

Her family would tell people later that Prema had handled the betrayal with grace and composure like they never would have been able to muster up themselves, never would have thought Prema capable of. Prema herself would add a few extra details whenever present for these retellings, speaking in a strained modest manner of the initial fury that made her throat constrict and her eyes burn, and a forgiveness that came almost immediately and without her summoning it.

But in that moment, if she were to tell it honestly, her mind had created a vacuum that wanted to close in on itself, and she felt herself unable to move, to get up and join her family now traipsing upstairs in single file, led by the righteous Mano, clucking, disappointed and about to don the full armour of Indian indignation. She knew where they would find Vimala, who would not be hiding, but sitting on her metal desk chair in the room they both shared, still next to her radio, legs curled under her and neck poised for the look of defiant shame she was about to present to her family.

Prema would say later that her family's admonishment was punishment enough for Vimala, and mollification enough for her. She would leave out the thoughts that occurred to her much later, that kept her awake at night, wondering if she might actually owe the win to the fact that it was not her name on that story.

But even if she had thought all that then, while sitting on the maroon rug, staring straight ahead at the radio while her family marched upstairs, her emotions did not present themselves to her as all that complex, but collided within the vacuum inside her head into one unified and crazy longing for a piece of paper and a Bic.

NEVER HAVE I EVER

NEVER HAVE I ever been so allergic to something in my life.

That is probably not technically allowable game play, but it is all I can think of as people go around the circle, taking turns to coax others into admitting all the outrageous things they've done. "Never have I ever had sex on a plane," says Radhika from India with a smirk, and there is the obligatory brief silence, before two people take a drink, and the group erupts into raucous, already tipsy, laughter.

I will win this game. I have done almost nothing—

salacious or otherwise—during my nineteen years on this earth.

One thing I have done, however, is discover that I am fantastically allergic to all manner of things, one of which is cat dander. The others are more interesting, including yellow food colouring Number 5, but it is the mundane feline allergy that is currently constricting my throat and lungs and producing a slight but alarming wheeze with every inhale.

I wouldn't even be here, if I weren't still ruled primarily by hormones instead of sense, despite my best hopes to the contrary. It is a boy—it always is—and the boy in question happens to be the owner of the cat in question. As luck would have it, I know the cat's name but not the boy's.

I don't know what breed of cat Louie is, but I should probably find out, for future reference, so I can tell doctors and other interested parties which type of cat affects me in the strongest and strangest ways. Typically, I feel an itch in my throat that ranges in severity, then I start making an embarrassing and horrible sound that I can only politely describe as "throat-clearing", and my eyes begin to water. A little asthma is not uncommon, but nothing that requires much attention, maybe one puff of my trusty Ventolin inhaler.

Today, however, I have already snuck off to the bathroom twice to rapidly puff away on the inhaler, and I am contemplating a third trip. The puffs temporarily convinced me, while I was still sitting on the closed toilet bowl, that I actually felt better. But upon returning to the group, seated in a haphazard circle on a couch and some bean bags, Essence Of Louie would waft up my nostrils. I imagined Ventolin the Valiant, waging a fierce battle with whatever it is in cat saliva that permeates the air and causes mass suffering, putting up a commendable fight even in the face of great opposition, before finally succumbing to his much more powerful opponent, waving the white flag and slinking back into the background of my bloodstream.

I know I should probably leave but I came with Clara, and I'm not sure I can find my way back to our dorm without her. I am terrible with directions and other spatial matters, and Clara is seated on the floor with a look of pure delight on her face, lapping up the game and the company of everyone around her, holding her rapidly condensing can of beer up as if ready with every round to admit to a statement and take a swig. But she never does. Clara hasn't done anything either, unless you count drinking underage, but I don't really, since it's only underage in the States, and we've been able to drink back home in Singapore for a year already. I never thought going to college in the land of the free would curtail any of my freedoms, but there it is.

It's one of the reasons Clara was so eager to come tonight, to this random house party in a run-down off-campus apartment shared by a few Moroccan and Turkish students. We'd gone to a school-sanctioned mixer for new international arrivals this morning, where we were expected to eat cookies, sign up at one or more of a dozen different activity groups' booths, and meet students and faculty interested in appearing "global".

I had already signed up for my activity of choice—the campus newspaper—at the regular activities fair, and was in fact carrying in my bag three copies of my first article (a fact I had perhaps reminded Clara about a few times too many). I thus focused my attention on the free chocolate chip cookies, America's greatest contribution to the world. While on my fourth, another foreign student, Tarik, asked us if we were going to the party later. We hadn't heard of it, of course, but as soon as it was intimated that there would be libations, Clara began talking as if it had been our plan all along.

I don't remember Clara as being all that much of a drinker back home, but I suppose you don't miss something until it's taken away from you. After Tarik left, Clara had squealed and promptly declared that we had to go. I was about to register a feeble protest that we hadn't come all the way to the States to hang out with the United Nations, when I glimpsed Tarik talking to another student I had not noticed before, who appeared to be manning one of the activities booths. He looked tired from having had to stand out in the hot Virginia summer sun all day, and his wavy hair was plastered against his forehead with sweat, but he still shot me a smile as he saw me looking his way. I turned to Clara and agreed to go.

And the evening would have been a perfectly tolerable one if 1) we hadn't been made to sit in a circle and play another infernal game, and if 2) the moment the one person of interest to me arrived, everyone hadn't pounced on his cat instead, cooing his name, petting and coddling him, making sure that his hair flew to cover every inch of the room.

To be fair to Louie, he is monstrously adorable—small enough to be scooped up in both hands, grey with large green eyes that seem about to pop out of his tiny face. But I have now lasted one hour and 23 minutes in this room, a record of some sort I am sure, and I listen to my breathing again, trying to decide if another Ventolin break is necessary.

I stop breathing entirely for a second when Louie's owner turns his eyes towards me, one hand still absent-mindedly buried in Louie's thicket of hair. He smiles and I smile back, confused, unsure if this is like a moment out of the movies, the pivotal point where our eyes meet that I recount forever to my grandchildren. Then I realise that almost everyone's eyes are on me, and it's actually my turn to play.

I debate the multitude of things I could say, while still acutely conscious of the fact that when I do speak, I may sound like a lung cancer patient. I could of course go right for the jugular and casually say, "Never have I ever had sex", which would most certainly cause a hullabaloo of some sort, but also be effective in causing several people to lose immediately. But then that's probably all these people would remember about me, that quiet brown-skinned girl who sat in the corner and kept going to the bathroom. Where was she from again? Mexico? Malaysia?

So I play it coy, and safe. "Never have I ever watched

a *Star Wars* movie," I say lazily, trying to make my voice soft and mysterious instead of barely audible due to oxygen deprivation. The predictable gasps ring around the circle, as most of the group take a swig. Clara, I notice, doesn't, but grins wildly at me. I shrug back at her. I have many more unbelievable statements in my arsenal.

I excuse myself to the bathroom again, and once there, shake my inhaler desperately before taking another puff, hoping it might somehow increase its effectiveness. I pull the flush at the same time as I take the puff, expertly masking the sound of my feebleness as I have so many times before, and make an auditory show of washing my hands so no one standing in line for the bathroom can judge me for poor hygiene.

When I open the door, a blonde girl rushes past me into the bathroom, muttering in another language, and Louie's owner is next in line. I quickly pocket the inhaler. "You've never seen *Star Wars?*" he says, and his face crinkles into an easy smile just like it had before.

His accent is unfamiliar to me, but with the overtone of an American twang, just like every other international student who has lived here for a while. "No," I say, and then before I can stop myself—as though I know this is the only reason I am still here—I ask: "What's your name?"

"Sam," he says, and reaches out to shake my hand. I hurriedly wipe my wet hands on the back of my jeans, too distracted by the sure knowledge that I will never find a "Sam" on Facebook and realising it would be way too awkward to inquire after his last name as well. "Myra," I say. "From Singapore," I add helpfully.

"Cool," he says, and doesn't offer any corresponding information, or maybe he doesn't have time to, because my next inhalation produces a clearly audible wheeze. We stare at each other for a second, his eyes questioning and mine beseeching him to let it go, before I force a laugh. "Sometimes I breathe like that," I say, and immediately wish I hadn't, but he laughs too. I notice Louie, who must have stalked in silently, curling his little body in a figure eight around Sam's legs and curse the cat inwardly for undoing all the effects of the surreptitious rescue inhaler mission in the bathroom.

Sam sees me looking at the cat and immediately becomes more animated. "You a cat person too?" he says, but thankfully does not wait for an answer. "I found Louie just yesterday, actually, on a trip downtown. He followed me into a coffee shop, and then to my car, so I just let him hop on in. I had a cat back home, you see—and he's just so cute."

"He's pretty cute," I agree. "So—you've adopted him now?"

"I guess," he says with a laugh. "I didn't really think it through, but once I got home, he made himself comfortable, and I didn't really feel like shooing him out. I left him at home today though and he made a mess, so I thought I'd bring him to this thing."

He bends down to pick the cat up, and Louie mews

and nuzzles into Sam's neck like they've known each other for years. Louie is closer to my face than ever before and I have to stop myself from instinctively taking a step back. "It's been sort of nice having him, actually," Sam says. "I've kind of missed having a pet for the past two years."

"So you're a junior," I say, hoping to turn the conversation away from cats.

"Yeah," he says, as the blonde girl flushes and darts out of the bathroom without washing her hands. "Well, see you out there."

I unwillingly take that as my cue to go back into the main living room, where the group has become more raucous and the responses less coherent. I claim my original spot on one of the couches again, realising for the first time that my heart has been hammering for the past few minutes. Someone is saying that never has he ever peed himself while drunk and the requisite *ewwwws* ring around the room before two sheepish faces take a chug and the mood disintegrates into screaming laughter again. I can't concentrate on anything happening here—my mind is still on Sam—but I'm still capable of being grateful that I am at least breathing a little easier now that Louie is standing sentry outside the bathroom.

It's Clara's turn now. "Never have I ever had a threesome," she says, in an unnaturally high-pitched voice. I roll my eyes as some people drink and others cheer. Clara has never had a twosome either, but I don't see her bringing that up.

Someone lightly touches my shoulder from behind.

"Myra, right?" It's Sam and I nearly forget to nod. "Could you help me with something for a second?"

He motions for me to follow him into the other room, where the bathroom is, and I do, trying hard not to appear too eager. We find Louie standing stock-still outside the bathroom door with his tail in the air and a look of extreme concentration in his eyes. He mews loudly when he sees us and the effort his tiny body is making to remain so rigid is adorable. If his presence wasn't so antithetic to mine, I might have entertained the notion of sitting down and scooping him into my lap.

"I'm not really sure why he's acting like this, but I think he might need to, you know, *go,*" Sam tells me. "He's not exactly house-trained—at my apartment I just have a makeshift litter corner lined with newspaper. Sorry to bother you with this—but what do you think I should do?"

I'm not sure how Sam got the idea from our brief interaction that I was some sort of cat expert, but I am reluctant to disabuse him of the notion as it seems to be the only means of our continued communication. "Well, cats are very clean creatures," I say, reciting something I once heard an old friend of my mother's say. "He probably doesn't want to go just anywhere. I think you should probably just set up a litter corner here. Or take him home, but I don't know how far away you live."

An ingenious way to ask where he lives! I congratulate myself momentarily as he considers.

"I think I'll set one up here. I don't know how long he

can hold it if he's just a baby, and he might be in pain," he says, sounding very serious. I feel a little of my attraction to him ebbing away, even as I observe in an almost detached manner his strong jaw, kind eyes and a latent smile I already know can make me change my mind. There's never been much love lost between me and animals—a trait I always worried meant I was a bad person—but I'd always assumed I wasn't alone in believing only elderly single women and children below the age of six wondered intimately about their cats' bodily functions.

"Okay," I say, wondering what to do now. It seems logical to offer to help, but I am already feeling the depth of my breathing decrease, and I have no desire to spend more time with Louie, let alone his excrement.

"I'll go find some newspaper or something, if you could—make sure he doesn't make a mess?" Sam says. I nod, even as I wonder how I could possibly prevent such a thing, and he leaves me alone with Louie, whose focused stare is now fixed on me.

"Hey kitty," I say, trying out my hitherto-unused cat-voice. "Hey, Louie. Hold it in if you can."

The cat keeps staring at me, or through me, it now seems, still unmoving, with its tail still pointing straight up. I begin to come around to Sam's opinion that the cat is in an advanced degree of discomfort. Either that, or Louie has recently become demon-possessed, a theory I am not entirely opposed to.

I hear Sam call for Ahmed, one of the Turkish hosts whose apartment we're in, and I hear them converse in a language I don't understand. After a while I hear Ahmed laughing, and then he says in English, "Just grab it, they won't notice."

Sam returns with a copy of *The Campus Chronicle*, and I inadvertently perk up, wondering if now is a good time to let him know that I write for that fine media outlet, and if this will perhaps open up a conversation about both our interests, upon which we will find we have many mutual passions and make plans to pursue them together at an indeterminate date in the future. Instead, he crawls into the bathroom and lays out the newspaper carefully, covering almost every inch of the tile. He looks up at me, almost to check if he's doing it right, and shrugs. "Best I can do," he says.

"It's great," I say, then feel dumb and amend it. "It's fine."

Sam gets up and then makes a grandiose show of bowing to Louie and gesturing him into the bathroom with a flourish. "After you," he says to the cat, and I laugh. I'm so busy laughing that I only spot the articles laid out on the floor after Louie stalks in. There on the bathroom floor is my first article and I open my mouth to point it out, but the laughter has depleted my already-struggling oxygen levels significantly, and I wheeze instead.

Sam looks concerned as I start coughing, and his eyes grow wide when I don't stop. He puts his hand on my back as he asks me what's wrong, and even through the cough-wheeze I'm stupid enough to relish his touch. "Inhaler," I manage to tell him, and he rushes out of the room. By the sound of the commotion in the next room, I can only

guess he has told the entire group that some girl is dying
of a coughing fit. I turn to see Clara run in and gasp, but
she understands and runs out again to grab my bag and
my inhaler.

When she comes back in and I am able to take two deep
breaths of Ventolin, I see Louie sitting on his haunches,
staring at me from inside the bathroom.

I turn away and rasp to Clara that I need to get some
fresh air, and to go home. "Should I call an ambulance?"
she asks, but I shake my head. I can talk more easily now.
"I just need to get out of here," I say, and tilt my head
towards Louie by way of explanation.

Clara helps me up, and the two of us walk into the
living room, where people are noticeably less concerned
than I thought they were going to be. I am both relieved
that I am not the centre of attention and miffed that they
had not cared more. I make a mental note not to attend
any more parties where my accidental death might not be
remarked upon.

"Hey, *Star Wars* girl," calls one guy I don't know.
"Where are you going? We're all drunk and you're not."

"That's the girl who almost died," slurs someone else.
"She lives!"

"She almost died? Shit."

Clara turns with a polite smile and starts apologising,
but I keep heading to the door, to fresh air, knowing this
guy won't remember my rudeness tomorrow, or even in a
few minutes. Once we get out, I inhale deeply—the still-
evident wheeze terrifying Clara afresh—and pull out my

rescue inhaler one more time.

I notice then that there are just two copies of the newspaper in my bag, when I had most certainly grabbed three (one for me, one to send home to my parents, and another extra in case either of the two aforementioned parties lost theirs). I check again hurriedly but almost immediately realise that Sam or Ahmed had probably seen the papers sticking out of my bag and grabbed one for Louie's makeshift "litter". I feel a sharp surge of irritation but I don't seem to have enough energy to be both pissed and breathing normally at the same time. I ask Clara how much of a walk it is to get back to our dorm.

I hear the door open behind us again and someone calling my name. I don't want to turn, but Clara does, and it's Sam, carrying Louie. "I just wanted to get your number or something, to see if you wanted to hang out again," he says. I feel Clara's eyes on me, and excitement radiating palpably from her body.

This is probably the juncture at which I should say no, call him a thief, or at the very least announce my debilitating allergy to his pet, but of course, I say: "Sure." My breath sounds shallow but he probably thinks that's just my voice at this point. We both get our phones out to exchange numbers. Louie purrs like a motor, and Sam laughs. "He seems to really like you. I thought we could do something next weekend, all three of us," he says. I smile, and glance at Clara, before realising he was talking about Louie.

He probably won't call, I tell myself as I type my

number into his phone, even as I also start wondering if pre-emptive antihistamines could be an option. I turn to walk back with Clara's face positively shining beside me and decide I must be some special class of self-loather to have a crush on a guy who just stole my first article to wrap his cat's shit up in, but what do I know? Never have I ever been on a date.

BODY ON BOARD

THE PEOPLE OF Phuket have stopped trying to learn English because it has been a long time since they have needed it. Most of the people who visit now are Russians, who don't speak a word of it either.

This helpful information is relayed to my six-year-old daughter Zara by Pop, a proud member of the English-speaking minority of the Thai populace, who is in the seat next to her on the Silk Air flight from Singapore to Phuket. He is the owner of a chain of boutique hostels, headquartered in Bangkok, but is now on a routine visit to the Phuket branch, where he is expecting to find every room occupied—as always—with Russians.

"They are everywhere," says Pop earnestly, looking from Zara to me and then back again, obviously trying to get my attention and ascertain my relation to the child he is regaling. I ignore him steadily. He turns back to Zara: "They come to Thailand, with not one word of English. Not one word! Even the Thai people know more English than them—they can at least say hello, how are you, do you want *tuk tuk?* This is crazy to me. I thought that everyone knows English nowadays."

Zara nods uncertainly and looks to me for some sort of cue as to what to do about him. Pop turns to look at me, too. "Hello, sir," he tries. "You have a lovely daughter."

His voice rises a little as he says the last word, with the slight hint of a question. I am aware that I don't look like Zara's father: my dark skin and angular features stand almost in stark contrast to my daughter's chubby fairness, but she doesn't look like her mother, either. Sometimes mixed kids just turn out like that. If you look closely at her eyes though, you can see they are actually just like mine: wide with a prominent lower lash line. I almost want to pettily point out this tiny similarity to Pop, but I manage to refrain from doing so.

"Thanks," I say and give him a tight smile that I hope conveys how unwilling I am to prolong this conversation. I smooth Zara's hair, check her seatbelt and adjust the kiddie neck-pillow she insisted on bringing, just to demonstrate my concern for my child plainly, so this stranger can't judge me when I fall asleep and ignore her in a minute.

I would normally have placed myself between Zara and any stranger on a flight—or my wife would have been on the same flight to sandwich our daughter—but the nature of this trip meant that I had to take whichever seats were left on the next flight to Phuket. It was lucky enough that I got two seats together, even if it meant being in the dreaded middle seats of the centre row. When getting into our seat, I'd initially thought a sour-faced man who had already yelled once at Zara near the boarding gate looked like he was going to sit in the same row as us. I'd made a split-second decision and placed Zara next to the rosy-cheeked, smiling man on the right aisle instead, leaving empty the aisle seat to my left, but he had kept moving. The seat to my left ended up being taken by a harried and pregnant Chinese woman, who boarded late and fell asleep almost immediately upon strapping in. I glance at her now, snoring softly, and wonder how awkward it would be to orchestrate a seat exchange to get away from Pop's chatter. I look over again at Zara. She seems to be fine, and really, I'm the one who needs the silence more.

The flight attendants have finished their cross-checks and are taking their seats, the plane is speeding towards take-off, the cabin lights are dim and I have pulled my eye mask down but Pop is still talking at an ever-rising volume, to keep pace with the din of the plane's engines.

"I just don't know how you will manage it," he is shouting, and I lift my eye mask to peer at him out of the corner of my eyes. He is shaking his head with an air of affected sadness. "Do you speak Thai?" he shouts, and

Zara shakes her head. "Russian?" Zara shakes her head again and starts tugging at my arm. I put my arm around her and I hope that sends a clear signal without having to break my pretence of already being asleep.

"My hotel is not very far from Patong beach," Pop tells Zara. "Do you already have a place to stay? My hotel is full but I can find you a room. And then at least you can have me to translate for you. Okay?"

He grabs a torn piece of napkin from the drink he had before take-off and fumbles around for a pen. "I will write you the address."

The alarm of having my accommodations altered forces me to give up the act. "That won't be necessary," I say quickly, pushing up my eye mask. "We're staying at the Marriott."

"You can change your reservation there," Pop insists. "I think my hotel will be better for you."

Zara finally decides she should put an end to this. "We have to stay at the Marriott," she tells him. "My uncle's dead body is there."

*

I received the news of my brother's passing rather unceremoniously, during my routine reading of the Sunday papers at 8am. In between news of a new school for the technically-inclined and an ad for hair loss, I spotted a short article with a name I recognised:

A 44-year-old Singaporean hotel manager was found dead in his residence in Phuket on Friday night.

Authorities say that Mr Prakash Gopalan, general manager of the Marriott hotel on the Thai island, died from a heart attack at least two hours before he was discovered. No foul play is suspected.

Mr Gopalan, who moved to Phuket eight years ago to take up his current position, lived alone in a property adjacent to the hotel. It is believed his body was discovered by a friend.

Hotel staff remembered Mr Gopalan as a jovial man.

"He was always laughing and joking whenever we saw him. He knew how to have a good time," said receptionist Aim Parnthong.

In a statement issued yesterday, Ms Fiona Allen, the hotel's head of marketing, said: "His energy will be sorely missed."

The Ministry of Foreign Affairs is appealing for Mr Gopalan's next of kin. Anyone with information should call 6319-5231.

I read this article a few times to ascertain that I had understood it correctly, and then once more to see if there was any possible way it was not referring to my estranged brother.

"Tricia," I said to my wife, who was sipping her coffee across the table. "It seems that my brother has died."

I heard myself and felt I sounded like a stilted character in a movie.

"Really?" she asked, not tearing her eyes away from her own section of the newspaper. "Hmmm."

There was no love lost between my wife and my brother,

so I didn't expect tears, but I was still a little surprised. I sat with the newspaper in front of me, staring at the page, thinking about who else I could call to share this information with, when Tricia finally looked up, startled. "What did you say?"

I pushed the page I had been reading towards her. "This article is about my brother. My brother died."

She made a grab for it, then read it either repeatedly or very slowly over what felt like a good half-hour. I had to resist the urge to shake her to tell me what to do next. "Oh my god, oh my god," she said when she finally spoke.

She looked at me searchingly and reached out to hug me, but I, for some reason, could not comprehend what she was doing and just stared at her. She settled for squeezing my arm. "I'm so sorry, sweetie. Oh my god," she said again. She had the beginnings of tears in her eyes and this made my heart rate spike.

"What do I do?" I said, feeling like a child.

"You need to give this hotline a call."

"What?" In the initial shock of reading the news I had completely passed over the phone number. "Yes, I'll do that right now."

The hotline must have been a dedicated one for Singaporeans who had discovered that their loved ones abroad were dead, because it was answered by a sympathetic-sounding woman named Angela who didn't at all get flustered when I stumbled my way through explaining who I was and the news I was calling about. She put me on hold while retrieving the information she had, leaving me with Josh Groban's "You Raise Me Up" as hold music, presumably to help me find the strength to press on. When she came back on the line, she sounded slightly confused, and asked if I wouldn't mind providing her with some details like my identity card number and my parents' whereabouts. "They've both passed," I told her, after reciting my IC number. "Is there a problem?"

"Sir, the MFA has been in touch with the Thai authorities about bringing your brother's body home," she said carefully. "But this morning, his wife contacted them as well, saying she would like to do the funereal rites in Thailand."

"His wife?" I think I laughed at this point. "Prakash— my brother—has no wife. He has an ex-wife but she— she's out of the picture. Is this a mistake? Or some kind of swindler?" Out of the corner of my eye I saw Tricia, mouthing *what wife* and I shook my head. This was clearly a mistake.

"No, sir, it says in our system that she showed the Thai authorities a marriage certificate, dated last year. But because MFA already put in a request yesterday, the authorities over there are holding the body at least until a next of kin from Singapore arrives to sort out the... matter," said Angela, who had transitioned from sympathy to awkwardness.

"I thought you were going to ship it back to me," I said, now feeling as though I were dealing with an errant Amazon delivery.

"Yes, sir, but now we can't. You will have to fly over

there. MFA will be able to help with the expenses," she said.

I sat in silence with this deluge of new information for a while with my mobile phone pressed almost painfully to my ear. "I'm so sorry, sir," said Angela, after the silence had evidently become too protracted. "Would you like me to make the travel arrangements?"

This struck me as ludicrous, and I wondered how much of this woman's job was like a travel agent's, making flight and hotel bookings, only that her customers were the saddest travellers in Singapore. "Yes, please," I told her. "I can leave tomorrow."

I ended up having to call Angela back to ask for one more ticket for my daughter. It was the school holidays, and my wife was still pulling long hours at work. Tricia insisted that Zara could not be left with anyone at all, not even my parents-in-law. Apparently, even a trip with her half-coherent father about to tussle over her dead uncle's body with an unknown potential gold-digger was a better alternative than any sort of baby-sitter. So Zara and I packed our bags. It only occurred to me at the airport that Tricia might be sending our daughter along precisely to capture this sort of scandalous detail and report them back with her childlike memory for mundane things.

*

Zara's announcement makes me cringe but at least it has the blessed effect of silencing Pop momentarily. He stares at her and then at me for an uncomfortably long time, so I nod awkwardly in case it is confirmation he needs. Zara turns to me, looking stricken, and whispers: "Was it bad to say that?" I shake my head and put an arm around her. "You're right," I say to Zara, but for Pop to hear. "We're bringing Uncle home."

I hear myself and feel I should have tried harder to sound convincing. The truth is that I am not sure at all that this body-collection mission is going to be successful. Who is this wife, and does she really have authentic documentation? If she does—and if she's Thai—she has a clear advantage over me in dealing with the local authorities in Phuket. All I can hope to do is show up bearing a strong resemblance to the dead man, produce some faded childhood photos I had dug up for this purpose, and then maybe throw myself on his corpse to prevent it from being buried on Thai soil.

"I'm so sorry, sir," says Pop, sounding sufficiently bad for having pestered us thus far into the flight. "Please, please, if you need anyone to help you speak Thai—let me know."

It appears it will be hard to rid ourselves of Pop and his linguistic services. I nod at him again and hope with all my heart that this will be the end of our communication forever, even as I sincerely doubt it. I glance to my left to see if the pregnant lady feels compelled to offer her condolences too, but she is soundly asleep. I feel an irrational wish to trade places with her, to be able to block out the world so easily, to be concerned with life instead of death, and to not be seated as close to Pop.

I pull my eye mask down again in a futile attempt to try to simulate the internal Zen I imagine my seatmate is experiencing. I know I have avoided being alone with my thoughts thus far, busying myself first with logistics, then packing, then getting Zara ready, and then fending off inquisitive strangers on the aircraft. But the feelings I am trying to avoid are creeping up on me, and I expect they'll all arrive the moment I identify Prakash's body: the realisation that my brother is dead, really dead, and that that means the thought I had always had at the back of my head—*one day maybe we'll get close again*—has to die too. And after that, assuming it all goes well with the wife, I'll have to bring his lifeless body home with me on a plane. Where will it even go? At the back of the plane? In the cargo section? Should I buy out a row of seats near me to rest the coffin? Will there already be a coffin waiting for me or is this a Styrofoam box situation? I feel my thoughts are turning ridiculous. I feel sure Angela from the MFA will have all the answers.

I suddenly regret bringing Zara along for the trip, even though my wife insisted. I had agreed because I thought she would provide a nice distraction, but now I feel keenly the prospect of having to process my own complicated feelings about my brother's death before wrangling his body from the clutches of a Thai wife and flying back with my hard-won cadaver, all with a six-year-old by my side, who will most certainly not stay silent and let Daddy "process".

She has already asked too many questions I don't have answers to—what happened to Uncle? Who is his wife? How come I've never seen her? Are you sad? Are you very, very, very sad?

Yes, Zara, Daddy is very sad, is my standard reply, but

it bothers me that I have to be asked that question, that I somehow am not displaying my grief the way other people seem to, that death the way Zara understands it right now calls for a reaction more pronounced than mine. I wonder, probably unfairly, if my wife or I have somehow given my daughter the impression that I'm not grieving, that I can't grieve for a brother I hardly saw, a brother I had nearly nothing in common with anymore, a braggart, a spendthrift, a lout by all accounts. Why do I even care so much about bringing him home?

I want to say, Daddy feels sad in a deep, deep way he cannot explain. But that of course would need more explanation.

*

Before my brother stopped calling—and I mean way before, before he became a serial womaniser, before his marriage broke up, before he moved to Thailand, before he became a high-flying hotel executive, before he was never in the same country for two consecutive weeks, before he started enjoying his liquor before lunch, before he moved out to live with friends, before our father left and our mother died, before he started caring what he looked like, before he stopped letting me hang out with his friends, before he started hiding magazines under his bed—before all that, we were best friends. I feel stupid stating that so baldly and obviously, in such a cliché, but it's true. It didn't matter that I was four years younger. He didn't think I was too childish or embarrassing to hang out with, to tell his secrets to, or to beat viciously in *Street Fighter.*

Almost everyone will claim to have this sort of golden phase with their sibling if they had a good relationship at all, so I don't want to pretend we were more special than anybody else. The phase ends, it becomes a fond and fuzzy memory in adulthood, and you redefine your relationship with your brother or sister through a different lens. Maybe I was the only one who thought it was a time that could come back.

When I think about my brother now, what keeps coming back to me is the day I started Primary One. We were in the thick of our golden phase then, and my brother had asked to be my class' prefect but hadn't told me. I was in a heightened state of anxiety about spending my first full day away from home without either of my parents. I also had my arm in a sling from having broken it a month earlier, and a new school bag I was unable to put on and take off without assistance. I realised this only when a teacher with a loudhailer directed us to form two lines per class and sit down. I turned around frantically, hoping my mother would still be there, but she had left, and as all my new classmates sat down around me, I was left standing, trying to wriggle out of my school bag with my one good arm, willing myself not to start crying on my first day of school. I felt my chest give a tell-tale shudder and I braced myself for the humiliation as I looked down at my classmates' questioning faces and then suddenly I felt the pressure of my bag's straps easing on my shoulders. I looked up and saw my brother with his gleaming prefect badge grinning at me like he had engineered the world's best prank. "This is how Ma does it, right?" he said, carefully taking my plaster cast out of its sling and the sling over my head before easing my arm out of my bag's left shoulder strap. I nodded, too overwhelmed with gratitude, too in shock that my brother could still be looking out for me here in school. He put my bag on the ground and told me he'd be back later to help me put it on before class. I clung to his hand to stop him from leaving and he laughed. "I have to take attendance," he said, pointing to the other classes' prefects doing the same. In a whisper, he added: "Don't hug me in school."

During my best man's speech for his wedding, I told a couple of stories, just regular, funny stories with a hint of nostalgia—an overblown fight we'd had when I took the last slurp of a milkshake we were sharing, how he used to let me go with his friends to the arcade after school because he was afraid I'd tattle, the shirt of his I'd stolen because a girl I liked complimented him in it. But I didn't tell this story. We had already grown apart by then, both of us knowing that he'd only chosen me for his best man because I'd chosen him first, and that I'd done it because it was tradition and I always played by the rules. I spoke too fast, didn't wait long enough for my punch lines to settle, and generally bumbled the speech but my brother got out of his seat to clap me on the back in front of everyone when I was done, and at that moment I felt a pang of something I couldn't describe. I wished I had included that story, and then I wondered if I should just tell my brother privately, but then what would that accomplish? I would end with,

"So yeah, you really looked out for me," and I'd look down and he'd look away and then we'd go back to the relationship we'd had as adults.

*

A stewardess sidles up to our row and asks Zara what she would like to drink. Zara's brows pull together and her mouth purses and her face goes into the expression I know so well which means that whatever this decision is, it will take forever. So I silently count to sixty—a minute is fair—while Zara thinks, orders orange juice, changes her mind immediately to apple, thinks while it's being poured, changes her mind to Coke, thinks while the stewardess (who has now cottoned on) just waits, changes her mind to Sprite. I then butt in to say I'd like a Sprite too, and just as both our Sprites are reaching our trays, I see Zara open her mouth again to say something and in a moment of great parenting I clamp one hand over her mouth while my other hand steadies the Sprite that's just been placed on my daughter's tray.

That's what I'm doing when the pregnant lady digs into my left thigh with nails like ice picks. At first I link the stewardess' look of horror with the pain, and think this lady is punishing me for what looks like child abuse, but I turn to her and realise she's the one in pain. "Sorry," she says in a strained voice, as I pry her nails out of my leg, only to have her clutch my arm. "A contraction. So strong."

The stewardess serving drinks gasps and rushes off to

the galley, while the few people nearby who have overheard are now exclaiming, but I can't make out individual words they are saying. I only hear the rush of blood in my own ears and the mounting fear of being part of something monumental but I glance back at Zara and calm myself down. She's not going to have a baby right now.

"This thing takes hours," I hear myself saying, and I sound stupid and callous. The lady is staring at me like I'm crazy so I parrot things I heard people tell my wife when she was in labour. "I mean, just stay calm. Take some deep breaths. Don't let these other people around make you stressed. This is probably just pre-labour."

"I know," she hisses at me. "This is not my first baby. But these are so strong. I don't remember them being so bad. I'm only at thirty-five weeks, and I'm not with my husband or my family."

Then she begins to cry, and the hubbub around us swells. The stewardesses now come flocking to her side, holding her other hand, offering her hot towels, asking if she'd like to walk around a little bit because we're still an hour from Phuket. "An hour?" she asks, through tears. "I don't know what to do."

I look over at Zara, whose eyes are wide and whose Sprite is forgotten; and Pop, who seems to be having the exact same reaction. Zara pulls at my sleeve. "Is she having her baby now?"

Her voice rises on the last word and I shush her hurriedly. "No, she's not, honey, but let's be extra nice to her because she's in pain, okay?"

Zara nods and tries to reach over me to pat the lady, in what I assume is a reassuring manner, but she can't quite reach and ends up just grazing the lady's elbow. The woman suddenly grabs Zara's hand and squeezes, which alarms us both, and I quickly substitute my hand for Zara's so that my daughter's fingers don't get crushed.

"Just try to transfer the pain to me," I say, because I remember saying it to my wife and I think she responded positively. The stewardesses have now left to bring more hot towels or perhaps just exclaim to each other about all the excitement, and I'm on my own. "Every time it hurts, just squeeze my hand. We'll be there soon, then they'll take you to the hospital, then they'll call your husband, and he'll get on the next flight over, the immediate next one."

Even as I say it, I realise this will be a multi-hour process, probably prolonged many times in the mind of a woman in labour.

"My husband is there, in Phuket," the lady tells me through clenched teeth. "He'll be at the airport. If they put me in an ambulance, can you tell him?"

I hesitate, not willing to suddenly take on all this responsibility for a woman who just happened to be sitting next to me on a flight when I have more important things on my mind than an impending baby. I have a corpse to fight over.

"I'm sure the airline people will call your husband if they put you in an ambulance," I say, but Pop cuts in. "I will inform him!" he announces eagerly. He's now leaning over

Zara, physically trying to block her out of the conversation. "There are not many in Thailand who can speak English," he says again, his tone valiantly maintaining a blend of pride in himself and sorrow in his people.

"He doesn't speak very good English," the lady says. "He's Russian."

Pop physically deflates. He's still leaning towards me but seems to be debating if he should sit back down. "Thai?" he tries.

I wonder if I should ask now how she had expected me to speak to him if he didn't speak English, but I don't think I should add to her current distress. "I'll handle it," I say, and my voice sounds tentative, but she squeezes my hand gently.

"Thanks," she says.

She seems to have calmed down a little, although I can tell from her face that that doesn't mean her contractions have stopped.

"Is there anything I can do to help you feel better?" I say, just to say something after a few minutes of sitting there in silence, Zara alternating between the in-flight games and staring at me to see if it was okay to ask something.

"Could you just talk? Keep talking," she says. "How much longer is this flight?"

I glance at my watch and decide against telling her it's just been ten minutes since she asked the stewardess. "Oh, I think we're close," I say, and try to gloss over my own obvious lie. "Well, this is my daughter Zara, she's six. Zara, say hi." I pause to let Zara give a little wave. I try to will her to talk now. *This would be a great time to start a little childish chatter and excuse your Daddy from having to carry on a conversation.*

But Zara remains mum, obviously under the impression that something horrendous is happening next to Daddy. "It's okay, Zara, this lady is okay. She's having a baby soon, isn't that cool?" I try to pry some interest out of her, and it seems to work.

"Is it a boy or a girl?" my daughter asks.

"It's a boy," the lady says. "My second boy. My first is with his dad in Phuket. I was just in Singapore for a bit visiting my family. I really didn't think he would be coming this early."

"How early is he?" Zara asks, evidently warming up to the subject. "And what is your name? And what is his name?"

The lady sort of smiles through her mask of discomfort. "My name is Anita. And I haven't thought of a name for him yet. Do you have any ideas? Do you have a brother?"

"I don't have a brother but I want one," says Zara thoughtfully and I suddenly feel like an inanimate telephone line linking them both by holding their hands, accidentally privy to thoughts they would only tell one another. "If I had a brother, his name would be Zachary. Or maybe my parents would name him Prakash."

I give a start, and they both stare at me, their telephone connection suddenly come to life. "That's not...she's just...that's my..." I say, apparently only able to speak in fragments now, and to my complete horror I feel tears come to my eyes. I let go of both their hands, breaking their connection, and get out of my seat, saying something vaguely apologetic, knowing they both have already seen my tears. I walk very quickly to the very back of the plane and stop just before the galley.

I just stand there for a while to compose myself, feeling like my tears don't match my internal state, which is more ache than upset. I don't know if Anita and Zara are still talking, if they are just holding each other's hands now, a direct connection. Maybe Zara has told Anita everything. Maybe Anita doesn't want to hear anything about a dead man because she's superstitious. Maybe Zara has convinced Anita to name her son Prakash, a random Indian name for a Chinese-Russian baby, and I close my eyes and allow myself to think about it all for a few seconds: Anita's baby, my arm in a sling, Prakash's body in Phuket, and how much I wish we could all start over.

REVELATION TO AMALA ROSE

WHEN AMALA ROSE burst into her house after running all the way from school to escape the noise that was echoing through the streets and found the rooms empty and her family missing, she thought the only thing she could possibly think: the rapture had happened.

She felt foolish for not knowing earlier. She had heard the brassy wail from the moment she had waved goodbye to Kavita after exiting the school gate and watched as her friend ran into her own house, where her mother was calling to her. The sound was persistent, alternating in amplitude—growing loud and then soft, then loud again—and Amala Rose had cupped her hands over her ears and run the whole 500 metres home, her backpack bouncing uncomfortably on her shoulders. There, she found the kitchen cupboards open, some of her mother's blouses strewn haphazardly on the living room floor, and her brother's toothbrush—still with toothpaste on it—on the dining table. Evidently God could not wait for them to complete household chores or take care of matters of basic oral hygiene.

This, of course, begged the most nagging question: why had they been taken up, and not her? As far as she could tell, her parents and brother were not that much more pious than she—they all went to St Thomas Orthodox Church every Sunday since they had moved to Singapore, recited the same liturgy, repented heavily and closed their eyes reverently at all the right places. She had been told repeatedly that she was saved, and did not need to worry about earning it, so why now this discrepancy? She started running through all the bad things she had done that her family might not have replicated, or ways they might have redeemed themselves that she had not. Was it about how often they read their Bibles? She ran to her father's bedside drawer and yanked it open, intending to make a last-ditch effort. His gold-leaf Bible, that the family read from after dinner every night, was gone. It would seem even the Good Book had been beamed up to Heaven, while Amala Rose had been left behind.

She despaired. The metallic wailing—which she now recognised as the trumpets of the angels in the Book of

Revelation—went on outside, and she could hear people running, crying and shouting for one another frantically. She wanted to go out and tell them it was no use: the chosen had already been taken.

How different it felt from just a year ago, when Appa had seen an advertisement for a job with the British Forces in Singapore in the newspaper one night and run out immediately in the dark to apply for it. He had returned with sweets and smiles, kissed them all on their foreheads and told Amala Rose that they were the chosen, the ones going to begin life anew in a small country, another British colony, where Appa would get a job and she would go to a better school. How difficult it had been to say goodbye to her friends, to stand by her mother as they assured the members of the Kokkamangalam congregation that they would locate and settle into the Singapore congregation at once, to choose just five out of her twenty special books so as to not weigh down their new hard suitcases. Now, she felt, it was all for naught. Would she have been taken up if they had remained in India? Had she been tainted somehow, by the long ship ride here, the days of school, the mixing with children of other races and religions? She thought guiltily of how she had pocketed Tian's pink eraser when she wasn't looking, of how she had sworn to Miss Wong that she had submitted that Maths worksheet and the teacher must have lost it, of how she had agreed with Kavita when she had said, "Your church is just like our temple, right?" No, Kavita, our church is not like your temple at all, she retroactively wanted to say, to set it right, to pronounce the words that might get her into eternity yet. Of course Kavita and her mother were still around— they were unbelievers, after all. They were probably still in their house near the school, stuffing their ears with tissue and wondering what on earth the sound was for.

She wondered what she should do now—should she resign herself to her fate and get comfortable, or still make some valiant attempt to get into heaven? If she were back in Kokkamangalam, she would have run through the village yelling to see if anyone else were still there, and seek comfort with them, or run to the church so she was at least the most religious of the abandoned heathens. But she was still shy around her new neighbours here, many of whom spoke only Malay or Hokkien, and she wasn't positive she could find her way to the local St Thomas on foot. She fleetingly considered running to the British government building where her father clerked—but then remembered he would probably have been taken up first among the faithful: there was no one quite as upright as her Appa.

She truly missed home for the first time since their ship had docked at Keppel Harbour and she had run from the boat onto the shores of her new homeland, unsure if she was confusing her relief at being out in the open with a sudden rush of love towards the new country. Her father, who had gone ahead of them, met them at the harbour to take them to their new home, a unit on the first floor of a shophouse next to a Chinese traditional medicine store that gave the street the permanent tang of ginseng. He had been so proud of it that Amala Rose and her brother had become caught up in his excitement, too, and barely thought about how much smaller it was than their house in India, how far it was from anyone they knew, how herby the air constantly smelled.

Of course, she'd heard her mother muttering under her breath every once in a while that they should have never left India—usually when customers for her tailoring business dried up—but Amala Rose only felt homesickness acutely now that the world was about to end and it appeared that she would shortly be facing judgement for sins unknown but evidently severe.

She now considered the possibility of running outside to join the other frenzied heathens, even if they did not speak the same tongue—they were alike in a more important way, after all—or even heading to Kavita's house to commiserate. But that would be resigning herself to her fate once and for all, so Amala Rose dropped to her knees in the middle of her small bedroom to make a final petition to God. She screwed her eyes tightly shut and tried to remember all the bits of the Bible she could, knowing that every wrong word could cost her eternity. She prayed fervently, if incoherently, and had just decided upon attempting the Nicene Creed in its entirety when a voice screamed at her to GET UP GET UP WHAT ARE YOU DOING?

She bolted upright, genuinely amazed that the Lord was still on speaking terms with her, when her brother grabbed her arm and began pulling her out the door, still screaming at her in apparent vexation.

She allowed herself to be pulled out of the house, comprehending nothing of what her very agitated brother was saying, but staring at him in wonder. She began running when he did, still not letting go of her arm, and the realisation dawned on her that the good Lord had not abandoned her after all, but sent back His emissary for her rescue.

She turned towards her red-faced, sweaty brother and wrapped her arms around him in sheer gratitude, causing him to trip. He looked like he was about to cry at the prospect of meeting their Lord Jesus when he yelled over all the noise JAPANESE COMING and she screamed back HALLELUJAH! Her brother groaned and picked her up before starting to run again and Amala Rose wept in relief and anticipation of eternity as the trumpets droned on and the distant whirr of aircraft glided into the symphony.

THE EMPLOYEE'S GUIDE TO TRANSPORTING CUSTOMERS TO MEXICO

ON NAPKINS:

When serving a dish to a customer, really look at the dish, examine its ingredients and ask yourself: is this a one-napkin sort of dish? Or might it be a messier dining experience? Only after full reflection on this point should you select the number of napkins you will present the customer, along with the cutlery. Most customers may not even notice, but every once in a while you will have a customer who will think to himself, "Wow, how nice of the waiter to be so thoughtful as to bring me nine napkins for these grilled prawns, for which I will obviously have to

*use my hands." Trust me, they will notice when you don't
bring them enough napkins, they will "tsk" noisily and
wonder aloud why in the world they were given only one
napkin for this messy burrito. But don't overcompensate
either, and just bring every customer a lot of napkins to
avoid thinking about each individual dish. You will have
customers angrily thinking just how messy of an eater you
must presume they are to need this stack of napkins for a
simple basket of chips. But getting the number of napkins
just right—this is an art that will distinguish you as a
waiter, and us as a staff, and that will be part of the X factor
that will give us an edge over our competitors, even in the
dog-eat-dog world of Singapore's food and beverage scene.*

Ria had harboured reservations about Guacamolay!
from the day she was hired. She'd seen a job ad online
with a creative font, looking for "spicy individuals" who
were "interested in Latino culture" for a job at a newly
opened "on the cutting edge of hip" Mexican restaurant
in Holland Village. She took a screen shot of the ad
and strolled to the interview in between dropping her
résumé off at a few other places that day, planning to cite
her teenage crush on Ricky Martin as evidence of her
interest in Latino culture. She ended up walking into the
restaurant and walking out with a job in five minutes.
She hadn't actually done anything, or even handed in her
résumé. The manager happened to be at the bar counter
when she had walked in. He had taken just one look at her
and screamed, *"¡Bienvenida!"* before immediately asking,

"Indian? Mixed? What are you?"

She was taken aback, but he hadn't seemed rude, just sort of earnest and enthusiastic, so she replied, "Indian. And mixed." Which seemed to be a good enough answer for him, because she could start the next day as part of a weeklong try-out period.

When she went in the next day, she found a dozen other faces like hers staring back at her: medium-tanned skin, large eyes, wavy hair, racially ambiguous. She felt slightly foolish stepping into the room, as all the newly hired staff stared at each other, recognising that it couldn't be a coincidence. The manager, a Chinese guy whose name turned out to be Dave, arrived shortly after Ria, and was the only person in the room whose ethnicity was clear. He hadn't shied away from the matter, but started the first of his many pep talks with: "As you can see, we are going for a uniform look for our staff, for the added layer of authenticity."

If Ria felt uncomfortable with getting a job based on her looks, it lasted no longer than the 15-minute bus ride home. She needed one, and maybe more than one, if she was going to afford to start veterinary school in Australia in six months. She went home and told her dad about Guacamolay!, adding tentatively that she seemed to have been selected for looking passably Mexican, but he barely lifted his eyes from his papers and grunted, "Your mother and I are proud." Which is what he still said to most things she told him about her life these days, never mind that her mother had been living with her new boyfriend in her native Finland for more than a year now.

On the second day of the job, Dave gathered the staff at the end of the day for a pep talk, which included a PowerPoint presentation with a vision statement, motivational quotes and sales numbers from their mere two days of work. The staff bore with it and smiled indulgently through IF NO ONE IS LAUGHING AT YOUR DREAM, YOU AREN'T DREAMING BIG ENOUGH! but they soon found out that the pep talks were a regular fixture of Dave's restaurant. They continued daily throughout the first week, and the entire staff had to stay back for an hour after the restaurant closed—an hour they were not paid for, but Dave insisted on.

Dave looked to be in his mid-twenties, with an unplaceable accent to his English that indicated he'd gone overseas and come back with lots of ideas about how to make a restaurant in Singapore just like some restaurant he had seen in the other place. In the middle of the second week, he announced that his managerial pep talks would now become a weekly affair instead of a daily one. The staff's sighs of relief were cut short when Dave pulled out a large cardboard box and dramatically opened it to produce A4-sized booklets bound by blue plastic rings all the way down the length of their spines. Dave distributed one to each of them, explaining that these were employee handbooks he had personally authored, and which he expected every one of them to memorise. Ria idly flipped through it while waiting to be dismissed and came across the section entitled ON NAPKINS, which told her she was not long for this place.

Dave ended the meeting—their shortest ever—with another one of his motivational quotes, splashed across the screen of the projector: WHEN WE ALL WORK TOGETHER, WE ALL WIN TOGETHER! He told them that there was nothing hard work couldn't accomplish, and that Guacamolay! was a concept just primed for success.

On the restaurant's name:

Some people may ask you why our restaurant is called Guacamolay! They may be referring either to the spelling or the fact that it has an exclamation mark attached to it. If they are asking about the spelling, please explain that the owner of the restaurant (myself) was concerned that many Singaporeans may be confused by the word "guacamole" and pronounce it accordingly as "guaca-mol". In order to avoid such embarrassment, I have given the restaurant an easy-to-pronounce name that sounds just like the delicious avocado-based food that we serve with every meal in the restaurant. If they are inquiring about the exclamation mark, please tell them (enthusiastically!) that it is there to convey how excited we are about our food, and how excited they soon will be, too, to have tried it!

On the exclamation mark:

Never leave out the exclamation mark in the restaurant's name, both in your written communications and when

*you say it out loud. If you say it without the exclamation
mark (with a lilt at the end of the word, a smile and some
excitement), it becomes just the delicious avocado-based
food that we serve with every meal in the restaurant. Please
remember that we need to keep up the image of our brand.*

Ria read the entire handbook *(The Employee's Guide
to Transporting Customers to Mexico)* while in bed that
same night, unsure if she should have reached the decision
to quit at the very first page. She predicted that she
would arrive at work the next day to mass resignations,
but funnily enough, everyone stayed, although they
never discussed the handbook amongst themselves. They
seemed to have lumped it together with the PowerPoints
and pep talks and other strange things Dave did that they
largely ignored. The latest of these he announced that
morning: all employees would be given Spanish names on
their nametags. Ria's name was mercifully spared: Dave
had thought about changing it to "María" for a while, but
later declared her real name "Hispanic enough". His own
Spanish name was Dario.

Despite being chosen for possessing a certain sort of
appearance, the employees of Guacamolay! were really an
assortment of ethnicities. They didn't broach the subject
for a week or two, but then someone suddenly broke the ice
and they all started asking each other. Used to a lifetime of
being asked "What are you?", the irritation of the question
made them avoid asking it of anyone else until put in the
bizarre situation of being surrounded by people with faces

as puzzling as their own. Most of them turned out to be
of mixed parentage like Ria, but only one other girl shared
her particular blend of Caucasian and Indian genes. Many
were part-Malay, some were Chindian, and only one could
boast actual Hispanic lineage. Cheryl/Carla was one-
sixteenth Spanish, a fact she brought up often. The other
employees felt it was too small a percentage to really count.

Their ages also spanned quite a range, from the 18-year-
olds in the kitchen to the 45-year-old waiting tables with
Ria, but it made no difference to their camaraderie. The
45-year-old, Hana/Ana, was a mum who had another job
and was taking evening classes to get a degree in business,
while the teenage twins with interchangeable names were
planning to work for six months and then travel the world
with the money they earned. A couple of others were like
Ria, taking gap years to save up for school. One man in his
thirties, Joel/Julio, was working in the kitchen to see if he
had what it took to strike out on his own with a restaurant,
and Cheryl/Carla was just passing time until she could
leave on a yearlong humanitarian project in January.
Ria had expected to have nothing in common with her
co-workers, thinking that they'd either be foreigners,
resigned to a lifetime of clearing tables in Singapore, or
people fresh out of JC or Poly, whiling away the time and
waiting to be struck by inspiration on what to do with
their lives. But everyone here had a plan, a goal which
the restaurant was just a stepping stone to; dreaming of
their lives post-Guacamolay! was one of the ways they got
through the day. She liked coming to work with these

people, thrust together through sheer coincidence of their appearances, and their company was enough to stop her from looking for another job every time Dave gave another employee presentation.

By the second month they were all close—a rag-tag bunch of Mexican approximates. It didn't matter that the restaurant was not doing great. They all called each other by their Spanish names and greeted each other in the morning with *¡Buenos días!* and a smirk. Joel/Julio occasionally let them snack on tortilla chips in the kitchen, and every morning started with the full low-down on the twins' various nightclub exploits or the latest bad behaviour of Cheryl/Carla's good-for-nothing boyfriend whom they all agreed she should break up with. The weekly meetings after closing were more bearable now that they were friends; they snorted openly during Dave's presentations and blamed it on a chair scraping across the floor, or exchanged whispered horror stories of their worst customers of the day.

On self-presentation:
As the face of our restaurant, waiters and waitresses are very important. Congratulations on making the cut! Please wear only the uniforms provided and make every effort to appear clean and neat. Women are encouraged to wear their hair in high buns, and the only jewellery allowed are large silver hoop earrings. Men are encouraged to slick their hair back with gel. Please learn how to pronounce every item on the menu correctly (a full list of the correct Spanish

pronunciations of all dishes is presented in Appendix A). It may be useful to memorise certain phrases, such as "Hola" (pronounced oh-la), "Gracias" (pronounced grass-yas), and "Es muy delicioso" (pronounced es mooi de-lee-see-oh-so). Under no circumstances will I tolerate a mispronunciation of the word "guacamole". I have already given you a pronunciation guide in the name of the restaurant! I also personally dislike people who mispronounce "quesadilla".

A review in *The Sunday Times* came out in the third month of Guacamolay!'s existence and it was not horrendous. It was mildly favourable, in fact, and Dave went insane with excitement. Ria walked in the following morning to find newspapers spread all over one of the tables, flipped open to the same page with the review cut out. She didn't want to ask what was going on, but as she bent to pick up the scraps littered all around the table, she saw that Dave had affixed the review to the centrepiece of the table, and not just this one, but every table in the restaurant. She bit her lip and decided to tell Dave that perhaps they could just put one on a bulletin board, or on a sign in the window, when she saw that he had done both already.

Cheryl/Carla was in the kitchen, slumped in a corner, massaging her temples. When she spotted Ria, she pointed behind her. Dave had also covered the employee notice board with copies of the review. "Does he think if we read it, we'll want to pay money to eat here too?" she asked. She took off her apron and balled it up, as though ready to throw it in like the proverbial towel.

Ria waited: this was a ritual, and they all took turns to do it. "It wasn't even that good a review," Cheryl/Carla continued in a more hushed tone. "Did you read it? They said we were 'above average as far as Mexican restaurants go'. What a glowing recommendation! *Dios mío*," she said, and then shook out her apron again and put it back on. Ria reached over to help her smoothen out the straps and tie them at the back.

But they couldn't deny that the review brought in customers. The team worked harder than it ever had, unused as they were to the rush. The increase in customers also meant more questions. Contrary to what Dave had anticipated in his handbook, the most common questions were not about the food, but about the staff themselves. Dave's attempts to pass them off as Mexican appeared to have worked too well, the Spanish names on their nametags being the final, convincing touch. Almost every day, one of them was warmly welcomed to Singapore by a customer, or asked why they had decided "to come such a long way to work". The staff convened an emergency employee-only meeting headed by Joel/Julio to discuss if they should tell the truth in these instances, or lie to keep up Dave's hard-won pretence of authenticity. They decided that Hana/Ana should bring it up at a meeting.

When she did, Dave was thrilled, and forbade them from telling the truth. He instituted a new rule: waitstaff should approach every new table by introducing themselves in Spanish, using their Spanish names. They spent the rest of the night memorising how to do this, and reading the

Wikipedia page on Mexico to pre-empt basic questions.

On making recommendations:
Every member of the staff should be able to make recommendations to any customer. Too often, I have been to restaurants and asked a waiter what their favourite menu item is, only to find out they have never tried the food. As such, the chefs will cook a different selection of dishes before every Friday's meeting especially for staff to sample (sample only please, we will not be cooking enough for everyone to have a full meal) and afterward, staff will be required to write down their impressions of the dishes and rank them according to their own preferences. Each week, with more dishes sampled, staff will be asked to re-evaluate their rankings. You are permitted to sort dishes into tiers. Staff will be randomly selected at each meeting to justify some of their rankings, and describe dishes as they would to customers. Descriptions of dishes should include knowledge of the cooking techniques involved as well as where the produce is from. Avoid overcompensating by over-use of words such as "scrumptious" and "mouth-watering".

*

Sales and customer figures were included in every Friday's presentation as part of Dave's plan to increase the employees' sense of ownership in the establishment. But even if they weren't, the way the tables started emptying out within a month of the newspaper review was a clear indication of the direction the restaurant was heading. Ria knew it, and so did everyone else. They started spending weeknights playing cards in the kitchen, and sometimes they'd even take off their aprons and sit chatting in the booths so that passers-by might think the restaurant had happy customers. Dave, however, was not gifted in this department, so they sat through six more weeks of his presentations on the restaurant's poor takings—THE HIGHER THE GOAL, THE HARDER THE CLIMB, THE SWEETER THE SUCCESS—before any sort of panic started showing in his eyes.

To his credit, he didn't break down that first night the panic set in. He went on with the presentation, then holed himself up in his office in the restaurant for the rest of the week. He would be there before the staff arrived and after the last person had left. That whole week, they didn't see him until it was time for the employee meeting. Dave showed up immaculately groomed, with a pressed shirt, hair slick with gel and eyes wild with no sleep. He started by apologising for forgetting to include a quote for this week's meeting, and the staff were sorry too, because at least it would have meant the very first slide didn't contain figures of the restaurant's insurmountable losses.

Dave soldiered on through the presentation, insisting that the fact he had placed the loss numbers in red, and the fact that they were so very large, was no reason to give up quite yet, that it was always hard for new restaurants, even one as stellar as Guacamolay!, and that the restaurant scene in Singapore was a tough one to break into, but it, like all things, was cyclical…

Ria exchanged looks with the rest as Dave finally trailed off and collapsed into his chair, which rolled comically away from them. Joel/Julio started reading off the numbers on the PowerPoint and making calculations out loud to distract everyone else, but it was a feeble effort in the face of a man who had just started blubbering noisily.

"It's over," Dave said, between angry sobs. "It's just over. I wanted it so much."

"Well, let's not give up yet," Joel/Julio said. "You know, they say it takes at least a year—"

"It's not just the numbers. There's something else I didn't tell you guys. All of us may be under investigation by the Government. I have no idea how it got so big." He buried his face in his hands.

Several people gasped as the room stirred uneasily. Ria's stomach clenched and her mind flew to the thought that this might stop her from leaving for school.

"I thought it was nothing at first, and I kept thinking it would be resolved, but I just got an e-mail that said someone had filed a complaint against us for *'discriminatory hiring practices'.*" Dave's use of air quotes showed what he thought of the grievance. "They say we have to be shut down for a week or so while the investigation is pending. With the numbers like they are right now, there's no way we'll make it through having to close for even a few days."

He stood up and screamed, "My dream is dead!" before collapsing back into the chair.

Ria wanted to shake him and yell: *This is all your fault, you and your stupid ideas, and now we are all out of jobs*

*and under an investigation! Why is your dumb dream
more important than mine?*

But instead she joined the rest of the waitstaff, who
flocked around Dave like his well-trained Spanish hens,
making comforting noises and reaching out to touch him.
"Ay ay ay," sighed the twins, while Hana/Ana patted him
on the shoulder and cooed, *"Pobrecito."* Ria swooped
down to hug him from behind and whispered into his ear:
"Que será, será."

On guacamole itself:

*Our restaurant is named after this delicious avocado-
based food that we serve with every meal, so it is imperative
we get it right. We will use only the ripest of avocados,
each of which will be tested personally by me upon the
arrival of each shipment. We will only bring in avocados
from Mexico, to maintain the taste of the first, true
guacamole I tasted during Spring Break '09 in Cancún.
They are more expensive but worth it, to distinguish
Guacamolay!'s guacamole from the other restaurants'
guacamole, and thereby distinguish Guacamolay! from
the other restaurants. If that sentence is confusing, read it
again. If Mexican avocados are in short supply, we might
use Australian avocados (in dire circumstances) but never,
under any conditions, Indonesian avocados. We will close
our restaurant if those are the only avocados available to
us. I will taste the guacamole prepared every day, to ensure
that the standards are high, and similar to those found
at the Grand Oasis Cancún All-Inclusive Resort. If I am*

unable to be there, Carla, who is 1/16th Spanish, will taste the guacamole in my stead.

Let us not let down the good name of our restaurant with bad guacamole. ¡Viva Guacamolay!

PG-13

We waited for Char to turn 13, even though her birthday was in September and movies we wanted to watch kept coming out all year. We made no effort to conceal our bitterness towards poor Char, who took the brunt of our ill-conceived pact to wait to watch a PG-13 movie until all six of us were officially teenagers. The pact forbade us to watch these movies with our parents, but I secretly succumbed when *Frequency* came out in July, and subsequently heaped a little less abuse on Char.

When we returned to school after the September holidays, we scoured the movie listings in the newspapers every day, but none of the films had the rating we needed. "There's nothing out in September," Lena would announce every day in the classroom as we put our bags down before morning assembly. She would stare pointedly in Char's direction, and we would all traipse down the stairs in glum silence while Char suggested in a falsely bright voice that the next day might bring new offerings. It didn't for a while, and then suddenly one Thursday, there it was: not a blockbuster, but a Hollywood movie all the same, one with an actress we recognised, and it bore the all-important designation: PG-13.

We were breathless that morning with excitement—and relief, for one of us—and made plans to watch the movie the next Friday, the day after a Lit test. We chattered about it non-stop that day, our unfair resentment towards Char finally dissipated. So I was completely blindsided when Lena cornered me the next day in the toilet and told me we had to kick Char out of the group.

"What, because her birthday is so late?" I asked.

"No, because she lies," Lena said calmly, as if that was that.

She was leaning against the door, possibly to prevent anyone else from coming in during this conversation, and I prolonged my hand-washing and drying to avoid responding. When the silence became too protracted I forced myself to speak, since Lena appeared to be unconcerned and checking her nails.

"What does she lie about?" I asked.

"Everything," Lena said, without looking up at me.

"About me to Rachel. About Tina to Shu-en. About you to me."

I felt a weight in my stomach. "What does she say about me?"

"Just lies. I know they're not true," Lena said, finally looking me in the eye. "And I know you don't believe the things she says about us to you."

She held my gaze as I evaluated the statement. Char did complain about the other members of the group to me, but I thought she had considered me her confidante. Her comments weren't all that vicious, anyway. Just little grievances—*Tina never contributes to group projects, Shu-en likes to show off, I'm not sure if Lena likes me.* They hadn't struck me as particularly slanderous, and certainly not outright lies—the last one, in fact, seemed like a legitimate concern—and I hadn't really blamed her. But I hadn't counted on her talking about me behind my back, and I felt a sharp surge of anger.

With Lena though, I had to pick my words carefully.

"We haven't been very nice to Char," I said, although the collective pronoun was exceedingly generous. "Maybe we could talk to her, tell her we heard these things she was saying about us, and then she can tell us to our faces what she's upset about."

Lena snorted. "Always the peacemaker, Priya. She's out there gossiping about us now and you want to sit down and talk. No, we're kicking her out. I've talked to the others, and now I'm talking to you."

I felt a bit miffed that I was the last of the group to

know, but I had more important things to clarify. "What about the movie then?"

Lena impatiently flicked her bangs out of her face. "Yes, that stupid movie. It's only because of that movie pact that we haven't done this earlier. We swore we would watch the movie together. Well, once that's done, the pact's done, and there's nothing really holding us together. If we'd kicked her out earlier we would still have to honour the pact, you know, and that would have been awkward."

Apparently, Lena took her vows very seriously. I wondered how long she had been plotting this particular move.

I stood in silence for a little while, wondering why no one had come to use the toilet, or whether someone had tried, but mistook Lena's weight against the door for it being locked.

"Do we need to do it at all?" I finally asked. "The school year is almost over. We won't see her for a few months, and when we come back to school she might be different."

Lena sighed as though she were dealing with a small child, and I sensed her growing frustration. I was torn between defending Char and preserving my good standing with Lena.

"Look, Priya, right now, we sort of know what she's been saying to people. We don't know what else she might say, especially to people outside our group, or teachers. If we make a stand now, kick her out, and let people know she's a liar, then when she does say something big, they'll know it can't be true," she said.

Then it became clear to me. Two weeks ago, Lena had snuck into Science Lab 3 to finish an assignment we were supposed to do the week before. We had stood guard outside the lab, artfully arranged along various pillars, to create distractions and alert her if a teacher was approaching. The next day at morning assembly, our principal announced that a Bunsen burner had been left on in Science Lab 3 all night—the fifth one in as many weeks.

"I just *cannot imagine* how any girl in *this school* thinks this is a funny prank," she screeched into the microphone, making all our ears ring. "There could have been a fire! There could have been an explosion! The school could have burned down. *Someone could have died.* I just *cannot imagine.*"

She then announced that a full interrogation would be made of every class that had used the lab the day before, and that the staff would not let up until the culprit had been caught.

Since our class didn't have a lab period the day before, we did not get questioned. The five of us who had been standing guard outside, though, knew that Lena had been working with a Bunsen burner and had left in a hurry, but none of us said anything about it that day, even among ourselves. She most certainly was not the serial arsonist the school was looking for, but we knew that if anyone suspected her of this last incident, she'd look guilty of them all. After school, Lena had suggested we go to the McDonald's near the MRT station. She'd bought us all

French fries, confirmation that we were in this together, and we would stay silent.

Char's growing estrangement from the group, though, posed a problem for Lena, as the witch-hunt was still on for the lab prankster.

I couldn't think of how to say I understood without making it clear what it was I understood, so I just nodded and immediately regretted it.

"Good," said Lena. "We'll do it right after the movie."

*

I had less than a week to defuse the time bomb that my group of friends had become. Every day, Lena would give me a knowing look and a slow nod, and I figured out after a while that she wanted me to nod back, a confirmation that I was still committed to the cause. I watched closely to see if she nodded that way at anyone else, but either she did it only when she was alone with one of us, or I was the only one whose loyalty was in question.

Every time I felt irked by that, though, I reminded myself that I was definitely torn. I wondered if I was the only one of the group feeling this crisis of conscience. Lena, clearly, did not see anything wrong with what we were about to do to Char, but surely at least one of the others did? I searched their faces all through class, but they looked the same, and would just smile whenever they caught me looking at them. I started to doubt that Lena had let them know of her plans, but couldn't think of a way to bring it up. It consumed my thoughts every day at school and I stopped paying attention.

In class, we often sat around circular tables with eight seats. No one ever tried to sit with us; everyone knew better. Most of our class was organised into groups like ours, solid cliques with firm boundaries that weren't taking any more applicants. The smaller cliques, with four members, would often share a table with another small clique, but those like ours were allowed to have two empty chairs. Even the independent operators, who cared about little other than their grades, would form a haphazard group of their own—a silent, studying clique. No one in our class had ever left their group, much less been kicked out, and it weighed on me that we would be setting the precedent.

"Where will Char go?" I whispered to Lena one day when we were the last two packing up after Maths. "During class. Who will she sit with?"

Lena took her time putting her things away. "She'll sit with whoever she wants to. It just won't be us, and it won't be our problem."

She hoisted her bag up to her shoulder and looked me in the eye. "Stop being weird," she said.

"I'm not," I said, taken aback.

"Yes, you are. You've been acting really strange since I told you in the bathroom. You're quiet and fake and during class you just stare at us. Seriously, stop it."

"Sorry," I said, realising I hadn't been subtle. "I'm just spacing out."

"Yeah, okay," said Lena, with more than a hint of suspicion. "We're already late for Science Lab."

When we got to the lab, Lena and I were the last to arrive and were made de facto lab partners. I scanned the assignment on the worksheet and saw that it needed a Bunsen burner. Lena had perched herself on her stool, not looking at the assignment, and was regarding me a little coolly, so I figured that I should probably count on being on my own for this one. As I took the burner out and plugged it into the gas supply, Lena's eyes flashed a warning to me, and at first I thought she wanted me to be careful with it, but then I saw it was another small test of my loyalty. It was the first time any of us had been with a Bunsen burner since Lena's incident, and she was warning me not to say anything, again. I knew how to pass: I pretended not to notice her expression, I kept up a quiet stream of chatter as we held test-tubes over the flame and watched liquids crystallise, and soon her face relaxed again.

This gave me an idea. I remembered my conversation with Lena in the bathroom, and thought about how her grievances really stemmed from not being able to trust that Char wouldn't betray her. I started wondering if there was a way to ascertain that Char wouldn't tell on Lena and pretty soon it consumed me. I had to know.

Char and I went home on the same bus fairly often. We had different extra-curricular activities: hers was netball and mine was drama, and they met on different days. But on Tuesdays and Fridays, we both headed back home right after school on bus 105.

I looked forward to the bus rides with Char. Sometimes

I would forget what day it was, and when I saw Char heading towards the bus stop, I'd feel a pleasant jolt of memory—*That's right, I have Char for company today.* On the other days, I'd bump into various people I knew at the bus stop who were taking the same bus. There were very few of them I really liked to talk to, and I'd have been perfectly happy sitting alone, but all of them would expect me to sit with them, as the rules of secondary school go. Bus rides with these girls usually consisted of some light chatting and heavy silences while we both stared out the window or racked our brains for another conversation topic. With Char though, that never happened. It didn't matter that we had just spent the whole day in classes together—we'd start talking as soon as we were out of class and wouldn't stop till one of us stepped off the bus.

That day, Char and I were, of course, talking about the movie. We walked out the school gate and instinctively reached up to remove our nametags. This was a common practice in our school, but I never did it until Char talked me into it. "What if," she'd said, "an old lady gets on the bus and all the seats are taken and you're asleep in one, and she takes down your name to complain to the school later? They'd make an announcement the next day, MISS PRIYA MANIAM OF SEC 1-3, PLEASE REPORT TO THE PRINCIPAL'S OFFICE."

I laughed with her, then shuddered, then started slipping my nametag into my pocket upon exiting school, like everyone else.

Char told me that she had read a review of the movie

with a spoiler in it, but she wouldn't tell me what it was. "It's supposed to be really good," she said. "Really strong themes. They say it's going to be nominated for an Oscar."

I felt sure she was just parroting the review, and perhaps trying to sell the movie a little more since it was her fault we'd missed all of the year's PG-13 summer blockbusters, but I just nodded. "I can't wait," I said, excitement mixed with dread in my stomach. I looked at Char, who was still chattering excitedly, the innocent lamb to the slaughter.

"My mother thinks the movie is too adult for us, but I reminded her, it's PG-13 and we're all thirteen, okay?" Char said. "She's still grumbling about it a bit, and she thinks that we're all watching it because Lena wants to. She thinks Lena acts a lot older than she is."

"She does?" I asked. We had reached the bus stop at the perfect time; 105 was just pulling up and I had managed to avoid eye contact with everyone else at the bus stop that I knew.

"Yeah, but don't you? Maybe she just has an old face. And I heard she wears make-up when she goes out. My mum says we shouldn't be trying to look twenty at this age," Char said as we showed the bus driver our bus passes and practically ran to the two empty seats at the back of the bus.

"I don't think she's trying to look twenty," I said, realising for the first time why Char was so entertaining to me. She really was always talking about other people—our friends. And I liked listening to all these things about them that I would never say, learning scandalous details, knowing that Char was telling me, by proxy, *you're* not like them. I started wondering then if what Lena and the others said about Char could possibly be true. How much of what she said could be verified? Or were they all so strategically juicy yet insignificant that I would never bother to check?

I started worrying that the group would think I was complicit in Char's crimes. I tried to change the subject. "What time is the movie on Friday, again?" I asked, even though I knew the answer perfectly well. "Will we have time to change out of our uniforms?"

"Yeah, it's only at three o'clock," Char said dismissively. "We can bring our entire wardrobe and change fifteen times if we want. As Rachel no doubt will."

Until I was consciously trying to stop her from doing it, I hadn't realised how much Char talked about the rest of the group in less-than-flattering terms, and I hadn't realised that I got a slight thrill from hearing them talked about while not participating in the gossip myself. Now I wasn't sure what she was saying about me to the rest of them. I still had to figure out a way to see how committed Char was to keeping Lena's lab mistake a secret, and tried to approach it vaguely.

"We have Science Lab for our last period on Friday, right? I hope Miss Woo doesn't keep us late. But the last lab was actually quite fun. Making those crystals with the Bunsen burner," I said carefully.

It was easier than I'd imagined. Char sniffed and immediately said: "You were partnered with Lena right? Did you make sure she turned off the burner?"

I gaped at her. "Don't say that so loud," I hissed, checking the seats behind and around us for anyone else in our school uniform who might have overheard. "Anyway, it really might not have been her at all."

Char snorted loudly. "Please. Why did she buy us all fries that day if not to keep us quiet? It was totally her." She made an attempt to speak more quietly, but her voice was still too loud for my liking.

I decided to come right out with it, as best as I could. "You didn't tell anyone, right?" I asked, trying to look casual about it, but probably failing.

"No," she said, looking straight at me, as though I should comprehend her meaning.

When I didn't say anything for a few seconds, she continued. "But I know Lena thinks I did."

"What?" I said, still careful to keep my voice down despite my heart starting to hammer.

"It's so obvious," Char said, turning away from me and towards the window as if she were bored. "She's been so cold to me since it happened. Even when we found the movie, I thought she'd be so happy and finally stop being mean to me about my September birthday. But she acts like nothing has changed at all. She barely looks at me or talks to me anymore."

"That's crazy," I said, not knowing how to respond but understanding instinctively that I had to deny knowledge of everything for the sake of self-preservation. "She knows you wouldn't say anything."

I heard my voice rise a little on the last sentence, and I

felt betrayed by my own vocal chords.

Char laughed. "I wouldn't have before. But now I might. Don't think I haven't noticed that things have changed. At first it was just Lena who was cold, but it seems lately like things with Shu-en and Rachel are strained, and a few days ago Tina snapped at me for no reason. It's only you who has really been normal, to be honest."

That's because I didn't know, I felt like saying. But instead I said: "You wouldn't really tell on Lena... Would you?"

"It depends," Char said evenly, meeting my eyes without flinching. "It depends on how she treats me. If this goes on, then I really don't know."

"But they'll kick you out," I said, the words spilling out before I could stop them. "They'll kick you out of the group, and then what will you do?"

Char bit her lip, but I could see she had already thought of it. "Well," she said. "You'll come with me though, right?"

*

My anxiety made its way straight to my stomach and I spent most of the night in the bathroom. My mother was worried about me, and I was tempted to confide in her and ask her what to do, but whenever I rehearsed what I was going to say, it sounded unbearably juvenile. *Lena wants to kick Char out because she's scared she'll do something and Char wouldn't have done it but now she might because of how mean Lena is being.*

I was also equally ashamed at my own alarm when Char asked me to leave the group if they kicked her out. I wanted to be a loyal friend, but I wanted to be a part of the group more. I liked all of them, even Lena, who was funny and smart when she wasn't trying to manipulate the group into excising a member. They were my friends too, and I didn't see why I should have to choose Char over the rest of them just because she considered me her one friend in the group.

The next morning, our Literature teacher was late for our first period and our conversation naturally turned to our movie, which was now only two days away. "What are you guys going to wear?" asked Rachel, interrupting Shu-en, who had just started to talk about the same review Char had told me about the day before.

Shu-en shrugged. "T-shirt and berms?"

Lena nodded and Tina said she was going to bring jeans. "And maybe a sweater? That cinema is very cold," she said, wrinkling her nose.

Rachel rolled her eyes. "I was going to wear a dress. But now I may not, since none of you are dressing that nice," she said, with a small pout. "But maybe I'll just bring a few options and see what you guys actually end up wearing on that day."

I didn't mean to catch Char's twinkling eye right then, but I did. She pursed her lips as though trying to suppress a smile but a small laugh escaped her. I wanted to laugh too, but couldn't risk it with Lena's eyes on me. Instead my face twisted into a half-smile half-grimace that was the furthest possible thing from the neutral expression

I wanted.

Lena caught up to me by the lockers. As she leaned against them, I briefly felt relief that at least we were not in the bathroom this time.

"So, you and Char. Are you best friends now or something?" she asked, sounding careful.

"No, of course not. Why would you ask that?" I shoved my books into my locker and made a huge show of jamming the lock shut violently. "Come on."

"You've been acting weird since I told you that we were kicking her out. You seem like you are always so worried about her. You share all these little inside jokes and giggle with her. You're being so defensive now when I'm asking you about her," Lena said, numbering off each point on her fingers. She stopped. "So. Are you a lesbian? Are you and Char lesbians together? Is that why you don't want to kick her out?"

I felt all of the heat in my body rush to my face. "No. Of course not. Are you joking? That's not a funny joke. That's gross," I said, alarm rising within me as I realised my protests would now be taken for further defensiveness. "I like guys, you know that."

"It's not gross," Lena said calmly, studying my face. "It's normal, you know. Nothing weird about being lesbian. A lot of them in our school, you know that, right?"

"Stop saying that word," I whispered, knowing I sounded like I was begging. "I'm not."

"Okay," said Lena. "Sure. So we're still on for Friday? We'll all talk to her after the movie. Give her the weekend to get over it."

She kept staring at me, as though daring me to disagree now that I was in her power.

I nodded. "Yes," I said forcefully. "The plan has been on this whole time. I'm in."

Lena walked away, pulling out her hair-tie to put her ponytail up a little higher. I watched it bounce and swing from side to side as if taunting me, and stood by my locker until the feeling of wanting to cry passed. I had no choice now, I told myself. I had to go through with it, or risk being branded by Lena and the rest of them, and *lesbian* probably wasn't the worst thing they had in their arsenal.

I thought so long and hard that my stomach started roiling again and my head started hurting. When I put my fingers up to my face, the heat of my embarrassment felt like a fever. So I started thinking about how falling sick right after the show would solve all of my problems.

*

I set my new plan into motion almost immediately. I had to really commit to it, so I started selling it to my parents that night. "Feeling pretty tired. I think I'm going to bed early," I told them at 8pm, and they were shocked enough to turn away from *The West Wing* to inquire if I was feeling all right. "I think so," I said heroically. "Good night."

The next morning, I made sure to be quiet. I started the first of many sniffles I planned to keep up till the next afternoon, and made sure that when I did talk, my voice would rasp halfway through a sentence.

Only Char noticed. "Are you okay?" she asked. "Hope you're not falling sick right before the movie."

"I wouldn't miss the movie even if I were on my deathbed," I told her, trying to make sure my rasping voice carried a little to be heard by the others.

Rachel noticed. "Priya, you cannot fall sick. You said you'd wear a dress with me tomorrow, right?"

I nodded, grateful she was at least paying peripheral attention to me. I kept up the act for the rest of the day, sprinkling light coughs throughout the Lit test we had in the last period, so that when I said after school that I was going to skip Drama and go home to rest so I'd feel better by tomorrow, even Lena looked sympathetic. "Will you be penalised for missing today?" she asked.

"I don't think so. I haven't missed practice yet this year and I think my mother can write a letter," I told her. "I'll see you tomorrow."

I made sure to croak on the last word.

Char caught up with me as I got to the school gate, and I realised I hadn't thought to wait for her since I don't usually leave right after school on Thursdays. "Oh hey! I forgot what day it was," I said, but her face told me this wasn't going to be an especially enjoyable shared bus ride. "What's wrong?"

"You know just now how we all passed our tests to Lena to collect them for our table and bring them to Mr Lim?" Char said, her eyes flashing with anger. "I just went back into the classroom to check if I'd left my water bottle, and saw my essay still on the table. She handed in everyone's but mine. I had to run to the staff room to find Mr Lim, and he was really suspicious of me, like I had purposely not handed it in to get more time. But if I hadn't gone back and seen it, I would have gotten a zero on it."

"It was probably just a mistake. It must have slipped out," I said, keeping my voice weak to disguise how unconvincing I sounded.

"It wasn't. I know it wasn't, and I hope you know too," she said.

I thought about it, but I couldn't decide. It could have been intentional, but taking a risk on Char's grades was a bigger act of aggression than just ignoring her or being cold to her in class. I wasn't sure that Lena had really meant to step up her bullying right before kicking Char out. On the other hand, if it were a mistake, then it was a really badly timed one.

We walked the rest of the way and waited for the bus in silence, before I decided I had to change the mood before it affected my long-awaited movie outing tomorrow. I started telling her about how I was learning Chinese from one of the PRC scholars in class, who sometimes rode 105 with me, but that all I had learned so far was *"ni mei you tou fa"*. She laughed hard and we tried to puzzle out why the girl would have possibly tried to teach me that, and I worried it was a comment on my hairline. She started telling me about her brother's new girlfriend, who really did have a receding hairline, and who was constantly trying to bond with her by talking about fashion and music that Char had no interest in. "She even bought me this small bottle of perfume," she said. "I don't know what to do with it. I mean, who wears perfume?"

*

On the day of the movie, not even the showdown at the end of the day could stop me from waking up feeling excited. I made sure to temper my enthusiasm, loading up on tissues for the sniffles I would have throughout the day and packing over-the-counter flu medications in the front pocket of my school bag, where I knew they could be spotted every time I opened the compartment to take my wallet out.

"Are you still going to the movie after school?" my mother asked as I ate breakfast at breakneck speed and started shovelling my things into my bag. "I thought you might not be feeling up to it."

"I'll come home if I get worse," I promised, knowing exactly at what point I would get worse. "But I think I can still watch it."

"Okay, have fun," said my mother. "I'm worried it's a little adult…"

At school, predictably, we couldn't stay on other topics of conversations for long. We checked and re-checked that we all had our ICs. Rachel had brought three outfits and over the course of the day changed her mind three times about which one she would wear. After our last period, we all surreptitiously double-checked our Bunsen burners before we rushed to the big bathroom on the third floor to change out of our uniforms, enduring Rachel second-guessing her outfit again as we did so. I felt self-conscious about exiting the bathroom in my own clothes while in school, but being part of the pack made it better. We got a mixture of curious and envious looks as we walked out, almost skipping, giddy with excitement. The mall with the cinema was fewer than two bus stops away, but we decided to take the bus anyway, because we didn't want to get sweaty. "We look childish enough as is," Rachel said, a pointed dig at some of the group's outfits she didn't approve of.

We went to the box office first to buy tickets, nervous that a 3pm movie on a weekday might somehow be popular, but the bored box office clerk told us the theatre was completely empty. She was about to issue the tickets, and then noticed the movie's rating and asked to see proof that we were all 13 or older. We tried very hard to contain our excitement as we produced our little pink cards and pushed them over the counter, one by one. I felt inordinately proud of myself, and I could tell the others did too. The clerk was not as impressed as we would have liked, and pushed our cards back with the tickets.

We were too early for the movie, so we went to the McDonald's on the same floor as the cinema to pass the time. Tina, Shu-en, Char and I started the laborious process of counting out our coins to see how much we could spend on lunch, now that $7 of our precious allowances had gone towards the movie. Rachel refused to eat anything except a $2 Filet-O-Fish, which someone had told her was the McDonald's sandwich lowest in calories. After a few minutes, Lena got tired of waiting for us. "Guys, it's fine. I have money. You all just get a burger each, and I'll get a few large fries for us to share."

This was an appealing prospect and I looked up quickly to see if I would be the only freeloader wanting to take her up on it. "Really?" said Tina. "That would be great."

I nodded. "If you're sure...thanks so much, Lena." Shu-en echoed it and we got up to go order at the counter, but Char kept counting.

"Char," I said. "Lena's buying fries. Do you want me to order for you?"

She shook her head. "It's okay, thanks," she said into the air, to no one in particular, but of course it was particular. She stood, scooping her coins into her cupped palm. "I have enough here to buy my own meal."

Lena stared. "Don't be stupid. I'm buying, we can all share."

"It's okay," Char said, her voice sweet. "You guys can share. More for you all."

The others were no longer interested, so it was only I who noticed that when we all sat down with our food, Char touched not one of the communal fries, even though we had plenty left over, and she didn't even dip her fries into our mayonnaise or curry sauce when hers ran out. Lena watched her like a hawk, her mouth a straight line and her eyes somehow harder.

We were asked to show our ICs again just before entering the cinema. Rachel groaned as though this was such a hassle and obviously we were old enough. We followed her lead and acted like it was a bore, but I was still smiling as I handed my card over.

The movie was a comedy about an adulterous couple who cheated prolifically on each other and then fell dramatically back in love at the end. When the one actress whose name we recognised dropped her pants in the back shed with her much younger lover, revealing her perfectly rounded buttocks, we pretended to be cool with it. "It's just a butt," said Shu-en. "Not like a PENIS or anything." We all laughed more uproariously than we needed to, which was okay since no one else was in the theatre. *We have all seen butts! And we are not uncomfortable at all with you saying "penis"!*

Three-quarters of the way into the movie, I suddenly remembered the confrontation scheduled for directly afterward. I had let up on my pretence of illness. I panicked and then gave a small cough. I waited a while to sniffle, and then coughed again. I made sure to obviously shiver. I reminded myself not to overdo it.

As the credits rolled at the end of the movie, we stood up feeling slightly uncomfortable but very grown-up. "I thought the directing was great," said Tina. Shu-en added: "The cinematography was spectacular." We all agreed that the casting could have been better, and that there was barely a need for a PG-13 rating, really.

As we headed down on the escalators, Lena started talking about how the meaning of the movie was really about honesty and truth and being a good person. We all exchanged meaningful looks about what was about to happen next, which was how we realised that Char was no longer with the group.

We looked around wildly for her, wondering if she could have gone ahead of us on the escalators, or if we had left her behind. We tried calling for her but we only attracted curious looks from passers-by. Rachel and Tina stayed on the lower floor in case she came down while the rest of us went back up to look for her. Shu-en went to check the toilets, while Lena and I went back to the cinema, which was as empty as when we had first walked into it.

On a hunch, I walked to the row we had been sitting in. A McDonald's fries packet, turned inside out and neatly folded into a rectangle, was perched on top of the folded seat Char had been sitting in. As I got closer I could see on it a crude but clear sketch of a Bunsen burner. I wondered if it would be too late now for me to feign a fainting spell and fall upon the seat, blocking it from Lena's view. I heard her sharp inhalation of breath behind me and still I wanted to protest that it didn't mean anything, that Char would never be so devious as to betray us when she knew we would all be occupied and then leave a malicious clue, but I found I had lost my voice.

TENALI RAMAN REDUX

RAMAN'S MOTHER HAD known he was of above-average intelligence even when he was only the age of two. Amutha's hunch was further confirmed as he grew older—precociousness in speech and an absurdly early ability to read was followed by an inappropriately wide vocabulary, a propensity for wildly complex mischief, and an uncanny knack for never getting caught in it. Everyone in Tenali turned a blind eye to it because Raman was top in his form every year at the local school, and then became the first boy from the village to win a scholarship to go to university in Singapore. Raman was extraordinarily intelligent, his mother knew, which is why it came as no surprise to her when he landed himself in prison.

Her friends rallied around her after it happened, coming round to her house every evening after they had farmed and cooked for the day, bringing her little titbits—Indian sweets, nuts, fruit, whatever they still had saved from the last time someone in their family had gone into the city. They would awkwardly pat her on the back, look away when her tears fell and comfort her by talking about the decided flaws in the Singaporean police force. Sundari Mami, who could read a little, somehow got a hold of Tamil newspapers from Singapore, and told Amutha that they were calling Raman "the smartest swindler in decades". This was some small comfort to Amutha, who did not doubt the platitude for a second, and didn't even feel she could have prevented the boy's fate in any way—his brain just worked too quickly. She thanked her friends with small smiles and hot tea, and tried after a while to turn the conversation to more ordinary topics—the new style of saris they had seen in magazine scraps from the city, the Americans who had come to the village a few months ago to install a new water pump and sprinkler system for each farm, the village mailman's wife who had run off with one of them, the impossibility of actually working the pumps.

Her husband, however, was not as resilient as Amutha, and retreated into a seething silence upon receiving the news about their son. His daily routine—unchanged in forty-three years—was abandoned in favour of sitting on the house's shaky veranda, smoking occasionally, shaking his head often, speaking to no one, and refusing all food offered to him by the alarmed Amutha. For her part, she tried to keep up with his daily chores in addition to her own—tilling the fields, plucking weeds, irrigating their small farm in the old way. Amutha was not a sophisticated farmer, and after scrutinising the new pumps on the first day and trying unsuccessfully to work them, she had resorted to her husband's usual method of flooding the farm with water from the well and hoping the crops would absorb what they needed.

The city police, who had first brought them news of Raman's arrest and conviction, came back a month later to conduct a search of Amutha's small house, explaining nothing but making vague references to money, linked to Raman's misdeeds, that was still unaccounted for. Amutha asked the youngest-looking officer—chubby, baby-faced, with a moustache struggling to grow—if there was any word from Raman. When he said no, she implored him to find a way for her to correspond with him. The police officer, perhaps caught off-guard, perhaps reminded by Amutha of his own mother two villages away, agreed, and returned a week later with a scrap of paper bearing a hastily scribbled address in Singapore.

Her triumph in procuring an address for correspondence was quickly squelched by her husband's flat refusal to write to their son.

"But he's all alone, in jail in a foreign country," she pleaded. "He's probably wondering why he hasn't heard from us, wondering if we are too angry to write or receive his letters if he were to write to us. It doesn't have to be long—just a few lines?"

Her husband didn't even turn his eyes towards her, but exhaled heavily and scratched intently at a mosquito bite on his leg, which she took to be an unfavourable response. She didn't give up, and would plead with him at every possible opportunity—when they woke up, before they went to bed, when she brought him food he wouldn't touch, when she asked him to lift his feet so she could sweep the veranda.

She was starting to waver and her husband seemed to grow more stubborn each day, until she broke his resolve unexpectedly by breaking her hip.

It happened quite unceremoniously, not in the midst of any chores or act of heroism, but simply on the way to Sundari Mami's house to discuss her despair of ever hearing from her son again, and intending to plead with the good woman to use her limited literacy to help in some way. She was climbing up the three stairs to Sundari Mami's front porch, unaware that her friend's least favourite daughter-in-law had scrubbed them moments earlier with a new mixture that contained, among other things, a large quantity of used cooking oil.

She slipped so quickly that she found herself surprised to be lying on her right side and gasped as the first sudden spasm of pain shot through her body. She stayed there, trying to process what had happened, trying to figure out what to do, wondering if she should just lie there until morning when she might summon up the energy to roll

over and walk home. She was spotted by Sundari Mami
fifteen minutes later as she glanced out the window by
chance, and who immediately ordered her least favourite
daughter-in-law to step gingerly down the stairs and carry
Amutha home.

*

Two months after his arrest, prisoner #2398—known
to the wardens as that quiet Indian boy, known to most
prisoners as that damn-smart Indian guy, known to his
cellmate as that arrogant Indian fucker who doesn't talk or
share his shit, known to his parents as Raman—received a
letter in an envelope with blue and red trim and a telltale
AIR MAIL stamp that was very familiar to him but that
he hadn't ever expected to see again.

Inside the envelope was a single sheet of thin paper,
written on one side with ink that seeped through to the
other. In messy, impatient Tamil script, it read:

Raman,

*I hope you are happy. You are a criminal. Your mother
and I cannot show our faces anywhere. Everyone in the
village says you have an excellent brain. Actually, you are
an idiot. Because of you, we are dying. Your mother has
broken her hip. The doctor from the city (600 rupees but I
could only find 450 and he said okay) said she must have
bed rest for six months. Now who will water the farm? I am
too old. Also I am paralysed. By the shame of having you for
a son. The crops are dying. And then we will have no food.*

So we will die. We thought we had a son who would make some money and send it back and then maybe one day we could move to the city. Unfortunately we do not have this son anymore. I am writing to you to tell you that you are an idiot. And also if your excellent brain can think of how to keep us from dying, this would be a good time to share with us. But I am not expecting much.

Father

Anyone watching Raman read the letter (such as the disgruntled cellmate, already upset that his own parents had not written to him, jealous of the books and snacks the wardens sometimes slipped Raman, resentful of Raman's unspoken status among the inmates) would infer, from the slow smile that spread over his thin lips and momentarily lit up his scrawny, dark face, that he had received immeasurably pleasing news, good tidings of great joy, and unmitigated forgiveness of all sins past and future.

Raman let out a laugh (a shockingly high-pitched, alien sound that startled the cellmate) and proceeded to fold up the letter neatly. He took out a writing pad of his own—a present from a warden—and began his own reply.

Dear Father,

How good to hear from you! I am very distressed to hear of Mother's injuries and your own troubles. I know that my words will sound empty to you, but I am very sorry for the trouble that you and Mother have been through. As ashamed as this makes me, I may have a solution to your dire circumstances. I pray you will not judge me too harshly, as I was only thinking of you and Mother, and this may be a way out of your hardship for the moment. Some of the money that I was alleged to have "embezzled" may or may not be locked in a watertight chest at the bottom of the well. I lowered it in there myself when I was back in Tenali last year. It may take a few weeks of drawing water to get to it, but I suggest that you get a trusted friend to help you, since both you and Mother are sadly incapable of such strenuous work. I again hope that you will not judge me for this, and instead view this kindly as a reconciliatory and (hopefully) atoning act of mine.

Please tear up this letter after you read it.

Your ever-loving son,

Raman

*

She was in pain as she was carried back to her house and dropped rather uncertainly on her bed, where she stayed, in pain, as the doctor came from the city, clicked his tongue, shook his head at her and gave her tiny pink pills that did little to eliminate the jolts that started at the base of her spine and radiated to the far reaches of her body, until even her little finger seemed to be rendered immobile.

She was in pain when her husband opened the long unused drawer, when she heard the laboured, clumsy strokes of an old fountain pen's nib against even older paper, when she opened her eyes briefly to look towards heaven and breathe a thank-you to the gods in between the spasms.

She was in pain when the village mailman brought the letter bearing the postmark from Singapore and the small, neat handwriting on the envelope—too much in pain to jump out of bed and snatch the letter out of her husband's hands as she would have liked to, too much in pain to clap and laugh for joy and raise her hands to the heavens in a dance, too much in pain to have noticed the excessively tattered state of the envelope, or that it had already been opened.

She was in pain as she cried from the shame of learning the letter's contents, as she vehemently denied its truth, as her husband stood awkwardly by her bedside, patting her shoulder, wearing a look that seemed to convey embarrassment and triumph and guilt all at once.

She was in pain when they arrived, within a day of the letter arriving, no sooner or later than she had expected them to, and yet her stomach sank and tears sprang to her eyes unbidden when the first tires screeched to a halt in front of their house the next morning.

She heard them, even from her bedroom, and closed her eyes and tried to imagine that they were lost travellers, or even more well-meaning missionaries, but once she heard them crowding around the well—the

familiar soft splash of the bucket hitting the water, the
creak the pump made if someone leaned against it, the
thump of a head knocking against the wooden post, and
the choice expletive that followed it—she knew it had to
be the police.

She heard her husband's flustered voice, talking rapidly
to the police, explaining, apologising, cursing, acquitting
himself of all blame, and the men joking around the well
about pushing another in, or climbing in themselves to
claim the treasure.

She heard the creak of the pump turn into a slow,
groaning crescendo as the men—at least three or four, she
judged, by the sounds of the grunting involved—turned
the wheel that started it up, a laborious process that the
missionaries hadn't counted on, and a job made harder
still by the rapidly rusting metal it was made of.

She heard this symphony of creak, groan, grunt, curse,
groan, squeal, pant, until it was broken momentarily—
trickle of water, yelp—and then continued in the same
manner before the final movement: a light, happy finale
in which the sound of water being sprinkled over dry
earth on the verge of cracking was interspersed with self-
congratulatory cheers.

She heard the commotion as the policemen calculated
how long it would take for Raman's mystery chest to be
glimpsed, and as she closed her eyes in despair, she had
the fleeting thought that perhaps her fields, at least, would
now be watered.

*

His mother had sat up for the first time since her accident on the day she got Raman's second letter, two months after her fall, two weeks after the police had searched the house thoroughly, started up the water pump no one could start, watered the farm, drained the well and climbed into it themselves in puzzlement to search for a locked, waterproof chest full of money.

The letter was just as tattered as the first, had also been opened, and smelled like it had been spat upon. It read:

> *Dear Mother (and Father),*
> *I trust your problem has been solved.*
> *Your ever-loving son,*
> *Raman*

REGRETTABLE THINGS

WHEN THE INSTANT message arrives at 6.30pm—**COME OVER PLS**—I close my eyes and will it to be something else. *My editor has a small question about the story I filed earlier. My editor wants me to cover an event tomorrow. My editor simply wishes to inquire after my health.*

I take my pen and notebook out of my bag, which I had optimistically started packing five minutes earlier, and try not to trudge over to his desk. I smile and try to look eager, like a news hound hungry to see my by-line on the front page. This is what I should look like, or so I've been told.

Gary spins around in his chair and doesn't waste any time. "So I'm sure you've read our story today on the guy who murdered his wife in Clementi while the kids were out," he says. "We ran one yesterday too. Really fucked up case. Guy tried to cover her on the bed with a blanket later, like maybe he could leave and no one would know."

He's watching me carefully, so I nod. Of course I'd read it. Everybody had.

"Yeah," I say. "It was blurbed on the front page."

He pauses. I realise I'm holding my breath.

"Jess," he says. "Why didn't you tell us you knew the family?"

My held breath drops into my stomach like a stone. I wish I'd thought of what to say before coming over to his desk.

"I don't know them that well," I say. How in the world did he find out?

Gary reads my mind as always, and shakes his head. "Brian saw on Facebook that you're friends with the daughter," he says. "Close?"

I shake my head. I'm not friends with any of my bosses on social media, but Brian had been a regular journalist until just two months ago. That's what you get for thinking your friends don't change when they get promoted to assistant editor.

"No," I say. "We haven't talked in years."

This is one hundred per cent true. We haven't talked since primary school, in fact. But a more honest person would also add that when Nithya and I were in primary school, we were extremely close.

"Still," Gary says, and that one word tells me all I need to know about the rest of this conversation. "You have a connection to the family. The family that has been stonewalling us and every other publication for two days."

For good reason, I want to say. Why would two siblings whose father just killed their mother want to talk to a newspaper?

"I think I remember them being quite private, in general," I say. Not only is this true, it is an understatement. In primary school, I was one of only two friends Nithya ever let inside her family's flat.

Gary immediately takes my vague explanation as yet more evidence of my lack of go-getter attitude. "It's our job to make private people, talk, Jess," he says. "And while the family may be private, the case isn't anymore. A man killed a woman, and the police are investigating. The whole country is reading about it."

He stops again. "I think there's more to this case," he says.

A hazy panic takes hold of me. *He's not a mind reader,* I tell myself. *Calm down.*

"It doesn't add up," he says. "A couple is separated for, what, years? The guy comes over casually, neighbours say it's not uncommon for him to come over. That's in our story today. So the couple had an amicable split, but not a divorce. Over what? We don't know. Then one day he kills her, runs off, but just goes right back to where he lives like nothing happened?"

Gary's still studying me, as though I might offer a clue. I pray I don't. We stand in silence for a while.

"Police say he put up no fight when they arrested him," he says finally. "They won't tell me more than that. But a source says he's saying a lot of weird shit."

I nod, and start writing everything he said down in my notebook, my pen shaking a little more than it should.

"You know what I think?" he says. "I think the guy had some sort of mental illness. A long-term, chronic one. Like schizophrenia."

I keep writing.

"Police won't tell us that," he says, more carefully now than before, if that were possible. "No one will tell us that till a psychiatrist testifies during the trial."

He waits for me to stop writing.

"But a family member can."

I take a deep breath. "You want me to ask them if their father has schizophrenia?" I say.

"I want them to verbally confirm their father has schizophrenia," he says. "Because you already know that."

Any control I thought I had of the situation slips out of my grasp, as does my pen, which now clatters to the floor. I bend down to pick it up, trying to steady my heartbeat, which seems to have raced ahead some place else and left my body behind.

"The family is very private," I say again when I stand up, and my voice sounds like a desperate whisper. "They'll never tell a newspaper that."

"That's why they're not telling a newspaper," Gary says,

and I don't know if he doesn't understand or understands perfectly. "They're telling a friend."

It may be career suicide, but I have to at least try to get out of it.

"I'm not sure I'm the best person for this job," I say, in the most confident voice I can currently muster. "I may be too close to the story."

I realise this is the exact opposite of what I'd said before—that I wasn't close to the daughter at all—and hope against hope that Gary doesn't notice. But of course, my luck is never that good.

"Jessica Joseph," Gary says slowly. "Are you a journalist?"

He doesn't wait for me to nod.

"Do you like this job?" he continues, almost casually.

No, I want to say. *I write about dead people for a living.* But I don't want to be fired, so I open my mouth, ready to be as enthusiastic as he needs me to be, but he cuts me off.

"Your job here is to get the story. And because you're close to the story, you're going to convince this family that news is going to get out anyway, and it might as well be told by the most sympathetic ally in the Singaporean media industry they will ever find. Got it?"

This time, he waits for me to nod.

*

Gary makes me go immediately to Nithya's family's flat in Clementi. My feeble protests that it was too late in the day to show up at a grieving family's house were dismissed with a wave of his hand and a disappointed shake of his head. The disappointment was, of course, that I'm not the sort of reporter to be ready at all hours of the day to stake out a murder victim's residence.

So I take a long taxi ride over, my stomach roiling the entire time, and I rehearse what I'm going to say when I get there. The language of death should be familiar to me by now after nearly two years on the job, but it still doesn't come as easily as I need it to. I've said at least one thing I regretted at every interview with a grieving family, and I can't afford to do that this time.

As we enter Clementi, it startles me how easily the directions come to me even after moving out of the neighbourhood 12 years ago—*straight here, Uncle, turn left at the Shell station, yes, near the kopitiam, not this building, the next one.*

Nithya and I lost touch after we went to different secondary schools, the same year that my parents decided to move to the other end of the island. But before that, we lived just one bus stop away from Nithya's family, and I had walked this route to her flat enough times for it to have taken hold in my memory, and for that memory to have taken on the sepia tone of nostalgia. At first, she hadn't invited me into her family's flat, suggesting every time that we stay in the playground, or walk to get ice cream from a nearby shop. I hadn't found it strange until I suddenly did, and then it was as if she sensed the shift too. When she finally invited me up to her family's flat, her mother warm and fussing over us to eat a snack, her brother desperate to play with us, her father awkward and distant,

I understood instinctively whom it was that she was trying
to shield me from. She never had to say anything to me, or
I to her, so that the first time her father locked himself in
his room and started screaming that the man reading the
Tamil news on TV was spying on him—while her brother
whimpered and her mother darted between calming her
husband through the door and reassuring me that nothing
was wrong—I grabbed Nithya's hand and squeezed it, and
we both knew that whatever this was, I was never going to
talk about it.

It was a conspiracy that had begun on the very first day
of our friendship. It was the first day of Primary 3, and
everyone was in a new class, sorted according to how well
we'd done on the final exams in Primary 2. I already knew
who Nithya was due to an administrative mishap at the
end of the previous year. I'd placed into the best class, and
had been able to be proud of it for a full week, before being
called to the principal's office with my parents during
the December school holidays and told the scheduling
just wouldn't work for students who took Tamil as their
mother tongue. "But we can put you in the second-best
class, and you'll be the smartest of all of them!" said the
vice-principal brightly. I nodded, already deflated, as my
parents argued. I wished they wouldn't make a scene, and
noticed Nithya and her mother, called in for the same
meeting, quiet as I wished my parents would be.

As each class formed two lines that first day before
going up to our new classrooms, I found myself standing
behind Nithya, mesmerised by the navy blue ribbon

knotted neatly around her ponytail. When we arrived at class and she turned around, I noticed she had a bandage over one eye. Some of the other kids were already giggling about this, when Nithya's mother arrived in the classroom. I immediately felt sorry for Nithya as their giggles intensified, realising that probably none of them had mothers who looked anything like this petite, dark-skinned lady with thick, curly hair hanging loose to the hem of her salwar kameez.

"Hello, Miss Wee?" she said, her voice surprisingly sweet. "I just wanted to explain about Nithya's eye."

The teacher's gaze travelled over to me, and upon ascertaining I looked normal, searched the room for the other Indian girl. Miss Wee got up uncertainly and started walking to the doorway, but Nithya's mother continued talking, loud enough for the class to hear.

"We went to a crocodile farm, over the holidays. She had an accident there, but the doctor said she will take her bandage off by next week," she said. "She may have some trouble seeing the blackboard, or with her work for just this week."

Miss Wee nodded, clearly taken aback by a conversation she thought should have been had in private. Nithya's mother smiled shyly, a contrast to how confident she had been so far. "I just wanted you to know what it was," she said, before waving goodbye to Nithya, and leaving.

Nithya's falling star suddenly burst into a supernova. She had been injured at a crocodile farm. To nine-year-olds, that could only mean one thing: a crocodile had tried to eat her eye. Miss Wee lost total control of the class as everyone burst into easy chatter. Boys started re-enacting what they imagined had happened. Girls now crowded around her, brimming with concern that had been noticeably absent before.

If Nithya was shocked by the change in her fortunes, she didn't show it. She caught my eye with her one good one across the room, and gave me a small, shy smile, before turning back to the others' attentions.

At recess, later, I caught up with her as we both walked towards the chicken nugget stall. "Did you really hurt yourself at a crocodile farm?" I said.

The directness of my question may have caused her to read a knowing look in my eyes.

"Yes," she said, with no trace of defensiveness. She then lowered her voice: "But not in the way people think. I was running and crashed into a tree."

I started laughing, both from the absurdity of the situation, and the delight of someone trusting me so quickly and completely. She started laughing too, and it was the first of many things she never had to tell me to keep a secret.

*

I walk through the void deck of Nithya's block and press the button for her floor as if on autopilot. I am struck again at how familiar and strange these motions simultaneously feel. The familiarity of the neighbourhood, the block, the buttons in the lift, almost lull me into believing Nithya would be familiar to me too, but the feeling comes to an abrupt halt when I arrive at her flat. The front door is open, but the gate closed, and through it I can see Nithya on the couch. She rarely posts pictures of herself on social media, but even without them, I feel sure I would have been able to recognise her immediately. The whole interior of the flat intensifies the senses of the familiar and the alien battling within me—there's a new red couch, but that dining table with the scratches on the legs is the same; I recognise an antique chest of her mother's that we had to be extra careful around, but the framed photographs on the wall are all different; the gate in front of me is a shiny, new-looking green-and-gold contraption with bars formed to resemble creeping ivy, but the heavy front door behind it still bears a dent that looks like a smile.

I stand in front of the open door for too long. I'm half-hoping Nithya will look up from the book she has in her hands and see me, but she never flips the page.

I smooth my hair and push it behind my ears. I straighten my skirt and adjust my handbag. *I'm going to get through this by being professional,* I tell myself. *I'm not here on a condolence visit. I'm here to get the story.*

"Nithya," I say, and my voice sounds surprisingly sure of itself.

She looks up and I watch as her face passes through detachment, puzzlement, recognition and surprise. "Hi," she says and gets up to come to the gate. She stares at me through the locked gate for a second. "Jess?" she says slowly, as if to make sure, and I nod.

"Hi, Nithya," I say, and I can't remember if I'd rehearsed what I was going to say to her in the taxi.

I should have prepared better. The words tumble out of me: "I'm so sorry for your loss."

I want to kick myself. It was one of the first things my colleagues on the crime beat had told me when I started: *Don't talk in clichés. It makes you seem inauthentic. People can always tell when you don't mean what you say.*

I expect Nithya to withdraw, but she just nods and unlocks the gate. I step inside and we both stare at each other for a few seconds. She's not quite the picture of grief, but close: her curly hair is pulled back in a ponytail, she's wearing pyjama pants and a faded NIE T-shirt, her eyes aren't red but darkened at the peripheries, as if weary of crying. Still, she looks just like the friend I remember from primary school, and I am overcome with an urge to hug her. I am suddenly acutely conscious of my chemically straightened hair, my overenthusiastic application of mascara, my carefully pleated skirt: all markers of how much time has passed. I assume I look almost foreign to her, but she says: "You look exactly the same."

"So do you," I say, relieved.

She half-laughs and shakes her head. "I don't even want to know how I look right now," she says.

I think briefly about protesting this politely, but remember again the directive not to be inauthentic. I change the subject. "Are you the only one home?"

She motions with a tilt of her head to the three closed bedroom doors. "Karthik is in his room. My aunts were here just now, but they just went out to get some drinks and snacks," she says with a grimace. "Always so hospitable, even in the middle of something like this."

I nod, unsure if I should roll my eyes along with her. I look towards the couch, and she invites me to sit.

"Have a lot of people come by already?" I ask as I sit down. I want to keep this conversation as normal as possible, for as long as possible. I have no idea how to tell her this isn't exactly a compassionate visit on my part.

"Yeah, I think so," she says. "I don't really know. Karthik and I have been in our rooms most of the time. I think some relatives from my mother's side came by, some neighbours."

"Your friends?" I say, and immediately catch myself as Nithya visibly tenses. "Karthik's friends?" I add, to take the focus off her.

"Some people I work with wanted to come, but I told them not to. I don't really want them in my personal life. I mean, I don't even know if I can go back to work after this, with everyone knowing everything…" she trails off.

"Where do you work now?" I say.

"I'm teaching," she says. "I have a Primary 5 class this year. At our old school, actually."

I feel a twinge of embarrassment that I did not know this. "Wow," I say. "I had no idea."

"Yeah, it brings back a lot of memories," she says. "And I don't have to ask what you do. I see it every day."

It always stuns me a little that people recognise my name from the newspaper, and the jolt is doubly severe when Nithya says it now.

"Yes," I say, struggling for something more to say. I settle for: "Unfortunately."

She studies my face. "Is that why you're here?"

My breath catches, startled by the very topic I'd known all along I had to broach. It was silly of me to think even for a few seconds that I had seemed to Nithya like a concerned friend paying her a visit because of her murdered mother. We hadn't seen each other in years, and she'd seen right through me from the start.

I let out the breath. "Yes," I say, and debate saying more, but decide against it. Better to keep this forthright.

She nods and looks away from me. "I thought so. Karthik was the one who first mentioned it, actually. We had some reporters in front of our block, and one of them somehow got hold of Karthik's mobile phone number," she says, and looks at me, as though I could divine how this happened. I shake my head, both to say I had no idea how, and to express my disappointment with some colleague of mine for ferreting out Karthik's number.

She sighs. "He was so out of it he didn't even realise the person on the other end was a complete stranger. I guess they must have asked him how he was, and he said 'fine' because that's just what he always says, you know?"

She pulls up a copy of the Local News section from underneath the end table and reads from the page it's already flipped to: "Online searches revealed that Madam Reena had two children with Mr Mohan, a 25-year-old daughter named Nithya, a teacher, and a 22-year-old son named Karthik, an undergraduate. When contacted, the victim's son said that the family was 'fine'."

She looks up at me. "It makes us sound like monsters. We're doing just fine after our father murdered our mother?"

I know what Gary would say right now. He would jump at the opportunity and say: "Do you want to set the record straight? We can do that right now."

But I can't. I don't know which of my colleagues wrote that story, but I can't imagine it's something I could ever have done, using the monosyllabic mumble of a grief-stricken person for a reaction quote.

I say: "That was wrong of them. I'm really sorry."

She stops for a second, and seems to lose some of the tension that I didn't realise she had been holding. "It was really horrible to see that. I couldn't stop reading it, you know. Just kept reading it over and over. And Karthik has been beating himself up about it all day."

I nod, wondering how much further my shame could possibly deepen at this point, and then remember I haven't even started the interview.

"Has he been in his room all day?" I ask.

Nithya nods. "He told me you would probably try to call me. He reads all your articles, you know," she says. "He said you only write about 'bad things happening to people'. So I asked him why you didn't call me when my ex broke up with me last month."

She gives me a weak smile to let me know it's okay to laugh, but I am past the point of being able to smile back.

The thought that Karthik faithfully followed the articles of his sister's childhood best friend and knew to expect my visit when tragedy struck makes me feel like dirt.

Nithya is studying me. "So, that's true, is it? About what you write?"

I clear my throat. "He's not wrong," I say, my voice catching on the last word.

She raises her eyebrows. "What a horrible job," she says, and the emphatic way she says it makes me shrink. It's a thought I have almost every day, but hearing her say it somehow underscores how objective the statement is. "I guess you don't have a choice in what you write about?"

"Not really," I say. "We get assigned different beats when we start and don't really get to switch until we've been there a while." Professionalism seems to have gone out the window at this point so I add: "It really is horrible. I would love to write about anything else. Literally anything else."

She looks confused. "There's a beat that's just about people who died?"

Kind of, I want to say, but instead say: "It's not supposed to be. It's called Crime, so it should be about any sort of criminal activity. But there's not that much crime in Singapore, I guess, so we end up spending most of our time writing about…people who died."

She pauses. "Not everyone who died, right?"

I try not to chew my lip as I struggle to find the right words. "No," I say. "People who died of unnatural causes."

Those were not the right words. They hang ominously in the air between us now, these words Nithya has probably only ever heard on TV or read in newspapers, now used to record her mother's death and file it away somewhere by impassive hands.

She nods slowly and I feel the distance between us start to expand again. "I guess I didn't know there were that many murders in Singapore."

"There aren't," I say, remembering that this was one of the first questions I had asked another reporter. "We write about accidents, natural disasters, things like that, too."

The death beat, I remember thinking when I'd first heard this exact answer, and it seems to me to be what Nithya's thinking now, too. Any familiarity or warmth I thought I had gained so far seems to be draining away in Nithya's face, and she is silent for a long time while watching me, as though deciding what to do with me. I can't hold eye contact, and look down.

"Regrettable things," she finally says.

"What?" I say.

"That's what your beat should be called," she says. "Regrettable things that happened yesterday. That's more accurate, right?"

I have no idea how to respond to this and just stare at her, trying desperately to squash the discomfort that has been so plainly written all over me since I arrived.

"Yes, you're right," I say after a minute, at the same time that she says: "I'm sorry."

"I have no idea why I said that," Nithya says. "I'm feeling very weird. Please don't write that I said that."

"No, of course not," I say, finally feeling an opening to steer the conversation towards what I came for. "Nothing is on the record yet. Maybe you could tell me a little more about how you've been holding up? And now… on the record, if you don't mind?"

The first question is always the hardest, I tell myself as I involuntarily end up holding my breath to see if she will answer or show me the door.

She sighs deeply and sinks back into the couch. "Exactly how one would expect I'm doing," she says. She gestures to her clothes. "I haven't changed out of these clothes in two days. I couldn't stop crying until this morning, and then now I just feel like… I don't know. I don't know what I'm feeling now. Tired."

I nod, wishing I had taken out my voice recorder instead of my notebook. I feel like an idiot, scribbling my friend's words about her grief as fast as I can across notebook paper. It strikes me as both ludicrous and amazing yet again that people open up about their grief to reporters.

"And Karthik?" I ask. "About the same?"

She shrugs. "You remember Karthik. I mean, I don't know if you do, but he's always been very quiet, very sensitive," she says and I nod. "He's been blaming himself. But more than the normal way I've been blaming myself, or my aunts have been blaming themselves. Very intensely. That's kind of why the article was so bad. As if he needed one more thing to blame himself for."

I nod, and proceed before shame threatens to take over and derail the interview again. "Is there a reason he's blaming himself so intensely?" I ask.

She hesitates, then nods. "Well, you know what happened that night, right?" she says.

"Yes," I say carefully. "But would you mind telling me again? You were out, right?"

"Yes," she says. "And Karthik was here playing video games. That's why he blames himself, mostly, because he was right here when Pa—my dad came over, he was sitting right here when my mother was making him tea, and they were talking. He had these—noise-cancelling headphones on. They were super effective, I guess. I mean, I don't mean that in a mean way—no one is blaming him but himself. He didn't even realise they were in her room, or hear any struggle. The next thing he knew, my dad was leaving without saying goodbye, which is not that unusual for him, anyway."

She takes a breath. "When I came home, I asked him where my mother was, and we both found it strange that she was in her room with her door locked. My dad had locked it from the inside. We banged on it and there was no answer, so I went and got the spare room keys and opened it. She was on her bed, like she was sleeping, but there was blood on her head, and on the lamp beside her bed."

She says all of this matter-of-factly, like she's said it before, but it's clear it's still hard to recite the details. She pauses and looks at me.

"How did you react?" I ask, hating myself.

She bites her lip as if trying to remember. "Karthik says

I screamed very loudly. He says it didn't really register for him until I screamed like that and my mother still didn't wake up. But I remember him shouting. The neighbour came to see what had happened and then the police were there. I thought I called them but maybe the neighbour did. And then I think the police must have called our relatives, because two of our aunts came over very quickly."

Her chest heaves slightly. "They told me I didn't start crying until the police left."

I nod and look down, scribbling more notes than I need to. It was very unfair of Gary to ask me to do this and my shame at being here becomes anger towards him. I knew Nithya's mother, too. Memories of Aunty Reena come flooding back to me as I listen to Nithya's retelling of finding her dead body, but I cannot cry. I have to do the job Gary sent me here to do.

But Nithya visibly softens when she sees me struggling to stay dry-eyed. "Do you remember her?" she says, and I nod.

"She liked you a lot," she says.

I'm tongue-tied, caught off-guard again in an intimate moment in a professional situation, and beg my brain not to mess it up. After a pause I say: "I liked her a lot, too. She was always so kind to me."

Nithya nods. "She was maybe too kind to some people," she says, with more than a trace of bitterness.

"The police caught him that same night?" I ask, almost grateful for an easy way to continue an interview that has only become more difficult with each passing question.

Maybe it's the first ten questions that are the hardest.

"Yes," she says. "Within the hour. He was just sitting in his room, apparently. He's been staying with my aunt since the separation."

"How long ago was that?" I had been wondering about this in particular—her parents had been together when I'd last seen them, and I had always thought of them as extremely conservative. I wouldn't have thought Aunty Reena would have wanted a separation given what that would look like to the outside world, particularly after everything I'd already seen her put up with.

"Not very long," she says. "Maybe two years."

"And was it because...he was violent?" I ask, surprising myself.

She gives me an unreadable look. "No, he was never violent until this happened. For some reason no one seems to believe that just because—" she catches herself and stops. "Sorry. It's just that I've been hearing some of my relatives say the same thing, that he had always been violent, but he never was, not towards us anyway."

She looks away. "I'm not trying to defend him."

"I understand," I say quickly, almost out of reflex. I get a flash of an old memory of Nithya trying to tell me something without coming out and saying it, and me telling her I understood. After being in cahoots for so long, even when I didn't understand, I would say I did. What I remember most clearly now is the relief on her face when I said it then, but it doesn't appear now.

"My mother actually didn't want the separation," she

says quietly, not making eye contact. "He wanted it. When he makes up his mind, it's hard to stop him, even though my mother did try."

This stuns me, and I write it down slowly so as to not show it on my face. I had few memories of her dad—he was quiet, and stayed inside his room a lot, and seemed shy the few times I said hi to him. Other than the times when I knew he was the cause of the commotion behind locked doors, it had been easy to forget he was there, to forget he was part of Nithya's life.

"Why did he want to leave?" I ask slowly.

She gives me the same look again, then frowns. "You're not going to write about my parents' marriage, right?"

"Um, no, I'll just mention they were living apart," I say, suddenly flustered by the question. "I was just asking, because, you know, sometimes it turns out to be...relevant."

Nithya looks shocked, and I'm sure I do, too, since I hadn't planned to say that at all. "My father did not hate my mother," she says forcefully, and I'm back to being held at a distance.

"I know," I say quickly. "I'm just trying to understand why—"

"Everyone is trying to understand," she says, throwing up her hands. "Don't you think I want to know, too? Everyone has been asking why he did it, why he would have done it—my relatives, the police, everyone—but I have no clue. Something made him angry, I guess. Unless he tells us, we're never going to know."

"Has he said anything?" I ask quietly, trying to sink myself back into the couch cushions so as to somehow be less obtrusive. "Has he said anything to the police about why?"

She shakes her head, and doesn't meet my eye. "The police said they can't get him to say anything," she says.

The police are lying to you, I want to say to her. At least, that's if Gary's sources in the police are to be believed. And then I pause. I haven't even considered the possibility that she might be lying to me.

I decide to try again. "Wow, he's said nothing at all to them for three days?" I say, trying to look and sound as sympathetic as possible.

She nods, and looks at me once before glancing away and then I know she's lying. For some reason, this emboldens me.

"Nithya, I remember your dad, and he wasn't a violent man," I say, and she seems to relax before tensing again at what I say next. "So I hate to ask you this."

We lock eyes for a second and I try not to read anything into hers. "Is it possible it had something to do with his mental illness?" I say.

Her face contorts suddenly, but not in the way I was expecting. I had been digging my nails into my palms anticipating anger, not fear.

"My father did not have a mental illness," she says quietly.

I try to keep my face neutral, like I was expecting this denial, even as my heart seems to free-fall through my body. "Nithya," I say, and I sound confident to my own ears. "I know he did."

She looks away from me and towards Karthik's closed door, and I do, too. After a while, she says: "I didn't know how much you remembered."

I nod. "I remember what he was like," I say.

"I can't remember what you saw, or heard," she says. "I guess it must have been enough. You always knew he had—that he was sick?"

"I knew there was some kind of problem that I wasn't allowed to ask about," I say and hesitate before going on. "He said something to me once that scared me."

She doesn't look surprised. "I kind of suspected that he must have, at some point. What did he say?"

"He said that the aunty at the kopitiam drinks stall was trying to poison him," I say. "It scared me and I stopped going there. It was only a lot later that I realised it probably wasn't...true."

I see from her face that this was worse than what she'd anticipated. After a beat, she nods and looks away. "I wonder how many people figured it out," she says. "But I guess not many of my friends ever met my father."

"That was why though, right? You never had many people come to your house...because of your dad?" I say.

Nithya nods again. "I don't know when that became a rule, it was just something we always did. My mother was so worried that people would find out, so Karthik and I became worried too, I guess," she says, staring down at the couch and picking at some fraying fabric on it. "Makes you wonder what all the worrying was for if something like this could happen."

"You couldn't have known," I say, wondering to myself if that were true.

She half-shrugs and appears to grow pensive. "Sometimes I think, I can't believe he did this, there's no way we could have ever imagined that he would do this, that's not the person we know," she says, slowly. "But other times I'm like, why the fuck was this guy even around us growing up? How could we not have seen the danger? Why did we tell no one?"

Her sudden anger shocks me. I stay silent, almost waiting for the anger to turn on me.

She meets my eye now. "And that's why you can't write anything about his sickness in the paper," she says.

"What?" I say. "Sorry, I don't understand."

"I don't want you to write anything about what you know of my father's *mental illness* in your article," she says, mock-exaggerating the words I'd used, as though it were just my crazy opinion.

My mind searches desperately for a way to get back on a less antagonistic footing with her, while also feeling the failure of my current assignment looming not far ahead. "I, uh, understand, but I mean, as you know, that's a very big piece of this current…puzzle," I say, cringing at my own fumbling. "Maybe if you could tell me why you don't want me to write that, we could try to—"

"Why isn't it obvious?" she cuts in, and her irritation at me is evident. "We protected him for so long. We kept his secret for so long, because my mother wanted to, even after the separation, even after it became clear he was getting worse. And maybe it was the wrong thing to do, but we did it. If it comes out now, it's like we did it for nothing."

I look down at my notebook and don't say anything. I realise with a shock that I've written SCHIZOPHRENIA in tiny, block letters in the top corner of my notebook page. But my knowledge of it is worth nothing unless she says it. I understand what she's telling me, while at the same time thinking, *Yes, you did it for nothing. You did it for worse than nothing.*

I suppose my face must be transparent if both Gary and Nithya can read my mind today.

"I know we did it for nothing," she says, and her voice sounds strangled. "And there are a million things I would change about what we did with his sickness if I could go back in time, but I can't. If it were up to me, Jess, I would have told everyone a long time ago, I would have made sure he got medication from the start and stayed on it, I would have wanted help from friends, family, neighbours, everybody. But my mother never, ever wanted anyone to know, even after he moved out. It was her way of caring for him, and despite what anyone thinks, he loved her for it. And now that she's gone, that's the only thing we can still do for her—continue keeping it a secret."

"But Nithya," I say, feeling corrupt, somehow. "It's not going to remain a secret forever. The police will get a psychiatrist in. It'll come out during the trial. It's probably going to be his defence."

"It won't be his defence," she says, sounding short. "He

barely knows he has it."

"Nithya, they already know," I say, trying to sound gentle and not desperate. "The police already know there's something not quite right with him. They will definitely have him undergo psychiatric testing, and it'll come out in court that he has schizophrenia."

She freezes and stares at me like I have just struck her across the face.

"You have no proof that he has that," she says in almost a whisper. "You can't write that. You can't write something that you only know back from when we were kids."

I choke out the words Gary wants me to say. "I have no proof, you're right. But I know. And the police will know soon enough, and then everybody will know. But if I tell the story, I'll tell it in the best and kindest way, Nithya. If I don't, then we don't have any control over the way other people are going to tell it."

I see her eyes take on more hurt than coolness. "So this is why you came?" she says.

"Nithya, my editors know," I say. "They just asked me to confirm it."

"So you agreed?" she says. "How could you?"

"I didn't have a choice," I say. "It's my job."

"Your job," she says bitterly. "When you got here, I knew it was your job, but I stupidly thought it was just half-job. I thought you were still half-journalist, half-friend."

She looks away and sighs. "I think you should go," she says.

"Nithya, I'm so very sorry to come here like this," I say. "I feel so bad and I never wanted to come. But please believe me when I say I would write this story in the most sensitive way. I would let you all read it beforehand, even though we're not really allowed to do that, and it's not something other reporters would do if they broke this story."

"But if we read it and we didn't like it, you wouldn't change anything, right?" she says. "You wouldn't take out things we didn't want you to say."

"I would try my best to make changes in order to make you more comfortable with the story," I say, but the look on her face makes it clear she doesn't quite believe me.

"You won't take out any mention of his mental illness, even if I ask you to," says Nithya softly. "I just asked you, and you won't do it."

"Nithya," I try again but she cuts me off.

"You think you're being a friend by telling our story in the most sensitive way? Why don't you be a friend by not telling our story at all?" she says and it's clear that she's seconds away from tears. "Why can't you all just leave us alone?"

I open my mouth to protest, but there's only so long you can argue for something you don't even believe in. I can't think of what else I could possibly say, so I stay silent and look down at my hands.

After a little while of this, I slip my notebook back into my bag. There's really nothing left for me to do now but leave. Leave an old friend who feels betrayed, leave to go back to editors who will see this as yet more evidence of my lack of talent.

Nithya notices me putting my notebook away. "Do you remember how we became friends?" she says, not meeting my eyes.

I nod, even though she's not looking at me. "In Miss Wee's Primary 3 class."

"No, how we became friends in the class," she says and finally locks eyes with me. "I had a secret, and you figured it out. But you kept it to yourself."

My face feels hot. "The crocodile farm," I say. *This has nothing to do with that,* I want to say to her.

She nods. "And I know all you figured out was that I wasn't attacked by a crocodile, or whatever. But you didn't tell anyone anyway, and you let me enjoy that popularity," she says. "But for some reason, in my head I felt like you had figured out even more, and you were keeping that a secret, too."

"I don't understand," I say. "You thought I had figured it out about your dad? On the first day of Primary 3?" "I know, it seems silly, but that's just how my mind worked at that time. We went to that farm because someone told us that crocodile soup could cure schizophrenia," she says, going back to not meeting my eyes. "It was about a year after we found out what it was that was making him act like he did. For years, my father refused to take medication for it, so we did things like this. Gingko biloba. Fish oil. Amla berries. Then it became weird stuff like crocodile soup. And even as a kid I knew my mother didn't want me to tell anyone."

"So because you couldn't tell anyone the full story of the crocodile farm, you felt like you were keeping a secret about your eye injury," I say, understanding.

She nods again. "Yup. But I convinced myself that you knew, I guess, so I could feel like I wasn't keeping secrets from one person," she says. "I know. Stupid."

"It wasn't stupid, it makes a kind of sense," I say and take a deep breath. "And it also made no sense for me to come here today like this. I'm so sorry, Nithya."

She sighs as if resigned. "I know. And like you said, it's all going to come out anyway."

"Yes. But when it all comes out, you and Karthik should feel free to hate the person who invaded your privacy and published this one secret your whole family fought so hard to keep for so many years," I say. "I don't want to be that person."

"Really?" Nithya says, looking at me warily. "You'll just not do your job?"

I let myself look around the house properly for the first time and nostalgia hits me squarely in the chest. "I know I haven't seen your mother in years. But I will miss her," I say quietly. "And I know this is the worst way for us to reconnect. But I hope when you forgive me, we can do it right."

I stand up, and just then Karthik opens his door. He steps out, looking like a cornered animal. "Hi, Karthik," I say. "I was just leaving. And I'm sorry for what my colleague did to you."

He stares at me for a minute silently. I wait for him

to either retreat or look angry. I'd forgotten how socially awkward he was, but can't decide if a smile would disarm him or be inappropriate. I settle for a small one, and after a beat, he gives me a small smile back. "Okay," he says.

Nithya stands up too. "Give me your number," she says. "And thank you."

I reach for a business card and write my mobile phone number on the back. "Sorry this is so impersonal," I say.

We stand there again, unsure what to do, made a little worse by Karthik still wordlessly watching us from the threshold of his room. I impulsively give her a quick hug and move away before she or Karthik decide it was the wrong thing to do.

"So I guess we'll be hearing from a couple more reporters then," she says as she unlocks the gate.

"Probably," I say. "Feel free to treat them way worse."

She laughs a little and then becomes serious. "So you're not going to write anything at all from what I just said?" she says. "Nothing at all?"

I can see from her face that I have the near-miraculous opportunity here to regain the trust I just threw away.

"Nothing at all," I say.

*

I walk to the main road in front of Nithya's block of flats, my heart and stomach locked in a peristaltic battle. The entire day might have been better if I had never gone to her house, but I still have hope that I've somehow emerged not having been a bad person. But the task of informing my editors still remains, and as I check my phone, I see three missed calls and several text messages from Gary, telling me he's still in the office if I have a story I can file tonight. I debate going home and calling him to tell him, but it would be better to get it over with in person tonight.

A sea of green lights approach as though to aid me: an abundance of empty taxis. *Must be my lucky day,* I think, mentally rolling my eyes. I hail one and get into its icy interior, the air-conditioner turned to full blast and the windows almost fogged up. I tell the driver where to go.

"So late still working ah, girl?" says the cabbie, clearly energetic and closer to the start of his shift than the end.

"Yeah," I say. "Uncle, can turn down the air-con?"

I pull out my phone again to text Gary to tell him that I'm on my way back to the office. I don't want to call him and have to answer questions.

Just then, a text message comes in from a number I don't have saved on my phone. It reads: "Karthik and I will both talk to you. Tomorrow morning. If you still want to."

I read and re-read the text and my fingers freeze over the keys on my phone. My eyes feel unfocused and my brain doesn't trust itself.

"Still cold ah, girl?" says the cabbie.

I shake my head, both as an answer to him and to get myself out of my reverie.

Tentatively, I type back. "Yes. If you're sure. What changed your mind?"

The answer comes back in a minute: "Crocodiles."

The taxi turns right onto the highway. Not many cars

are out and I can tell the taxi driver is enjoying going fast.

It happens within seconds: A taxi going the other direction drifts into our lane right in front of us and I see its headlights and the faces of the other driver and the passenger beside him. The blare of the car horn rips through the taxi as I shield my eyes with one hand and grip my seatbelt with the other. The tires make a screeching sound I've never heard in my life and I feel the seatbelt strain as my body is jerked to the left and then to the right. The horn is still ringing in my ears as I realise the driver and I are still in the taxi together, intact, unhurt, moving forward with nothing ahead of us.

The cabbie's hands are shaking and mercifully a shoulder lane appears where he pulls over. He puts his head on the steering wheel as I take a deep breath and stare straight ahead. I turn in my seat to look behind me expecting to see a crash, but the other taxi is a speck, almost out of view. I realise that instead of pushing down hard on the brakes as many people would have done, my taxi driver had swerved into the lane of oncoming traffic and then swerved back into his to miss the other taxi narrowly.

He's crying a little now and I put my hand on his shoulder. "Thank you, Uncle. You saved our lives."

He looks up and his face is wet and red. He lets out a string of what I assume are Hokkien expletives. He gets out of the taxi and takes a few pictures of the stretch of road and the location markers around it on his phone before getting back in. "That idiot. I'm going to LTA to find his license plate from the video cameras and then I will sue him," he says.

"Are you okay to drive?" I say.

"Yes, yes. We're almost there. Nothing happened to me, right? But I'm going to sue him. We can both sue him, girl." He looks at me. "Why you like never react, like that?"

"I did," I say quickly. "I was very scared."

But the truth is that I did not, and as the taxi driver starts driving again slowly, I can still feel it, that lack of reaction. Even having survived it, I can't say I knew at that moment that I would be okay. I saw the headlights of a vehicle coming towards me in a head-on collision. I heard tires screeching and horns blaring, and I had covered my eyes and gripped my seat belt almost reflexively. It makes no sense that I didn't react as the driver did, and I sit in his back seat, feeling numb.

Three more texts from Gary come in, of course, and I don't read them. The cabbie keeps looking at me in the rear-view mirror. He sighs and shakes his head often, and I do the same when I catch his eye, but it's clear he knows I'm performing the motions for his benefit.

"What do you work as, girl?" he asks finally, after five minutes of driving in silence. "Why are you working so late?"

"I'm a reporter," I say. And then, on a whim, I add: "Crime reporter."

"Ah," he says. "That's why."

I nod, and almost laugh. "That's why," I say and it strikes me as both absurd and true at the same time: that perhaps the chief benefit of this job is that when death finally does come for me, I will be largely unsurprised.

ACKNOWLEDGMENTS

Thank you to Epigram Books for taking a chance on me. Thanks in particular to my editor, Jason Erik Lundberg, for mentoring me in 2014 and telling me to send him my collection manuscript when I finally had one; also for always enjoying my stories so whole-heartedly and making sure I knew it.

Thanks to all my friends who read my many drafts over the years—Steph Barnett, Yasmine Yahya, Magdalen Ng and Bailey Morton. A special thank-you to Mun Yuk Chin for bringing her professional eye and personal enthusiasm to "Regrettable Things".

To all of the VONA/Voices fellows for fiction in 2016—thank you for being so generous with your encouragement and advice. A special shout-out to Sharda Sekaran and Darise JeanBaptiste for your willingness to help me with my stories at extremely short notice and the thoughtful, detailed suggestions you gave me despite the deadline I gave you! I am so lucky to have writer friends who treat my stories like their own.

A huge, impossible-to-overstate thank-you to Tayari Jones, for your sharp story sense and incisive feedback that completely changed my title story, for teaching me so many things about fiction writing in a short time, and for how firmly you've been in my corner ever since we met. I am so grateful to you!

Thanks to my parents-in-law, Charley and Sara O'Hara, for giving me your laptop when mine stopped working and literally ensuring this book got finished. Thank you for always supporting my writing every chance you had!

Thanks to my dad, Durai, who first told me the Tenali Raman stories that inspired "Tenali Raman Redux".

Thanks to my little sister Rubhi, the inspiration for my very first short story, in which a perfect and oft-maligned older sister is finally vindicated when her younger sibling is not allowed to go to the seaside. Sorry about that…

Thank you to my mom, Vara Hariharan, for being a smart and intuitive beta reader and an even fiercer fan of my work. She holds on to things I wrote when I was five because she believes she can sell it as "juvenilia" one day. I'm thrilled that this book will be officially launched during her 60th birthday week, which means it counts as her birthday present. Right?

And the biggest thank-you to my husband, Chad, who was totally cool with me obsessively trying to write a book for more than a year, reads every word of every draft with academic levels of concentration, thinks all my characters are secretly based on him, and says I'm his second favourite writer after JK Rowling. Thanks for loving my stories like I do.

A note on "Tenali Raman Redux": this story is based on the folktale "Tenali Raman and the Thieves", one of the tales of Tenali Raman, a court jester-poet from 16th century India. Many tales are still told of his legendary cleverness and wit. One day, he spied some thieves lurking in his garden, waiting for him to go to sleep so that they could break into the house. He thought about how he could use it to his advantage and called out loudly to his wife that due to a spate of recent house break-ins, they should hide all their valuables deep inside the well. He then brought a box from inside the house and made a great show of lowering it into the well. When he went to bed that night, the thieves ran into the garden and began drawing water out of the well, pitying Raman for his stupidity and rejoicing that he had made their job so much easier. The thieves spent the entire night drawing water from the well, which they then poured into the garden, watering the plants in the process. When dawn was about to break, the thieves were still working tirelessly and the well was almost empty. Raman came out of the house and called out cheerfully to the thieves that they could stop now, as the whole garden was quite well irrigated by that point. The thieves heard this and ran away.

ABOUT THE AUTHOR

Jennani Durai is a former journalist, a VONA/ Voices Fellow for 2016 and a co-author of the official commemorative book of Singapore's 50th birthday, *Living the Singapore Story* (2015). Her fiction has appeared in venues such as *Hayden's Ferry Review*, *Eastern Heathens*, and the second and fourth volumes of the *Best New Singaporean Short Stories* biennial anthology series. *Regrettable Things That Happened Yesterday*, her debut collection of short fiction, was shortlisted for the 2018 Singapore Literature Prize for Fiction.

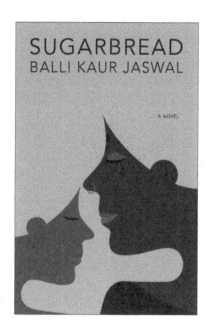

Sugarbread

BALLI KAUR JASWAL

Pin must not become like her mother, but nobody will tell her why. She seeks clues in Ma's cooking when she's not fighting other battles – being a bursary girl at an elite school and facing racial taunts from the bus uncle. Then her meddlesome grandmother moves in, installing a portrait of a watchful Sikh guru and a new set of house rules. Old secrets begin to surface, but can Pin handle learning the truth?

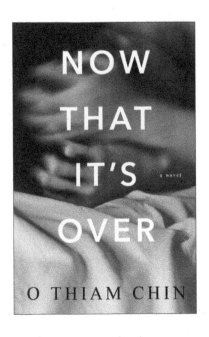

Now That It's Over
O Thiam Chin

Two couples from Singapore are vacationing in Phuket when the devastating 2004 tsunami strikes. Alternating between the aftermath of the catastrophe and past events that led these characters to that fateful moment, *Now That It's Over* chronicles the physical and emotional wreckage wrought by natural and man-made disasters.

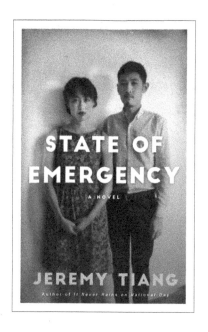

State of Emergency
JEREMY TIANG

A woman finds herself questioned for a conspiracy she did not take part in. A son flees to London to escape from a father, wracked by betrayal. A journalist seeks to uncover the truth of the place she once called home. A young wife leaves her husband and children behind to fight for freedom in the jungles of Malaya. *State of Emergency* traces the leftist movements of Singapore and Malaysia from the 1940s to the present day, centring on a family trying to navigate the choppy political currents of the region.

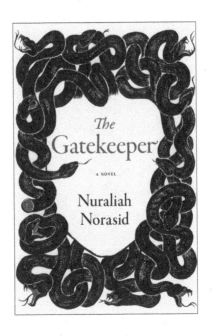

The Gatekeeper
NURALIAH NORASID

A 10-year-old medusa girl named Ria petrifies an entire village of innocents with her gaze. Together with her sister, she flees to the underground city of Nelroote, where society's most marginalised members live. Years later, the subterranean habitat is threatened when Ria, now the gatekeeper of the realm, befriends a man from the outside.

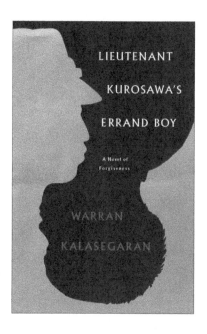

Lieutenant Kurosawa's Errand Boy

WARRAN KALASEGARAN

During the Japanese Occupation of Singapore, an eight-year old boy, separated from his father, is forced by his new Kempeitai boss to mimic his cruelties. When the unbelievable happens – Emperor Hirohito's 1945 radio broadcast of Japan's surrender – how does the lieutenant, the former striding victor now vanquished, rebuild his shattered life and seek forgiveness from the boy he brutalised?

Kappa Quartet

DARYL QILIN YAM

Kevin is a young man without a soul, holidaying in Tokyo; Mr Five, the enigmatic kappa, is the man he happens to meet. Little does Kevin know that kappas desire nothing more than the souls of humans. Set between Singapore and Japan, *Kappa Quartet* is split into eight discrete sections, tracing the rippling effects of this chance encounter across a host of characters, connected and bound to one another in ways both strange and serendipitous.

Nimita's Place
A K S H I T A   N A N D A

It is 1944 in India, and Nimita Khosla yearns to attend
university to become an engineer, but her parents want a
different life for her. As she accepts her fate and marries,
religious upheaval is splitting the country and forcing her
family to find a new home. In 2014, her granddaughter,
molecular biologist Nimita Sachdev, flees the prospect of
an arranged marriage in India, but finds uncertainty in
her new home of Singapore, where she faces rising anger
against immigrants.

The Art of
Charlie Chan Hock Chye
SONNY LIEW

In 1954, a young Charlie Chan witnesses a police attack on a peaceful student demonstration, an encounter that will eventually lead him on a quest to become Singapore's Greatest Comic Artist. This internationally-celebrated graphic novel traces his journey amidst the tumultuous times of pre-independent Singapore through to the hyper-modern metropolis the island city-state is today.